To Charlie
with love from

Christmas 1976

THE SHORN SHADOW

THIS exciting new novel is woven around a brilliantly-portrayed central character, Miguelito, who, at the height of his fame as a matador, abandons the career in which he has made a colossal success and a considerable fortune—and leaves Spain for England.

His decision to run from the shadow of the horn is a complicated one. A very strong influence on his life had been the elderly Englishwoman who taught him her language and deeply impressed him with the English dislike of bull-fighting.

Although in no way like *Juan in America*, this book might well be sub-titled *Miguelito in England*, for it is the incongruity of an innocent Andalusian in London which gives the novel its special flavour. England is suddenly seen in a new light in Spanish eyes. Try as he will, Miguelito, with all the superstition of a bullfighter, cannot escape from the shadow of the past, and he returns to Spain to resolve his dilemma in dramatic fashion.

PETER de POLNAY

———

THE

Shorn Shadow

W. H. ALLEN

LONDON

1956

Printed by The Garden City Press Limited, Letchworth, Hertfordshire
for the Publishers, W. H. Allen & Co. Ltd., Essex Street, London, W.C.2

To
ANTONIO GONZÁLEZ RIVERA

CHAPTER ONE

A BALD-HEADED anxious man with an unlit cigar in his mouth hurried towards a tavern in Seville. It was already November yet the heat of the summer hadn't gone. The anxious man darted from shade to shade, keeping his bulging black eyes focused on the pavement, and thus he nearly ran into a party of afternoon revellers. The number of the revellers was six: their leader, facing them, danced to the rhythm of their clapping. He was singing:

"En Sevilla hay una casa," and that cheered up Manolo, the anxious man.

"En la casa una ventana."

That was better and he decided to light his cigar. He was temperamentally superstitious and at the moment extremely worried. But in Seville there was a house and that house had a window. Nothing could be better and more to the point.

"Y en la ventana una chica . . ."

Manolo could have laughed at his fears. The girl in the window was the horrible, all-important Lolita, and as long as she stayed in the window there was no reason to be apprehensive about the future. At the street corner he left the revellers, whose singing and clapping was submerged by the clanking of a tram's bell. Behind his cigar Manolo appraised a passing woman's buttocks, then darted into the tavern to which he was summoned. The man behind the counter was leaning forward, staring at

7

a thin, slight man of about twenty-eight years with a pale though far from white complexion.

"Matador," shouted Manolo, "here I am. At your orders, matador."

His fear returned; for why did Miguelito want to see him in that obscure tavern instead of meeting him in the Andalucia Palace or in Lolita's house? Miguelito's eyes, which were prone to be sad, now met his, and Manolo looked away. There was, he often said, too much in those eyes; and Manolo liked other eyes to be only the reflection of his own.

"You needn't scream the word matador so loudly," said Miguelito. "They all know who I am. They told me so several times."

"They should," said Manolo slapping Miguelito's shoulders. "Everybody in Spain and in the world knows that you are the greatest matador since Joselito el Gallo, Juan Belmonte and Manolete."

"And two of them were killed by bulls," said Miguelito. "Besides you know that opinions about Manolete differ."

"He had few variations in his art," said Manolo sitting down, relieved, and ready to enter into technical conversation. "Bring two finos," he yelled to the barman. Miguelito said only one; he wasn't drinking; but Manolo persisted; and sadly Miguelito gave in. "But you have many," said Manolo relighting his cigar. "Your *natural*, your *pase de pecho*, your *molinete*, your . . ."

"*Molinete*," said Miguelito. "That isn't art and you my manager, you know as I know that a *manoletina* isn't art either. Nothing is art except the *natural*. When I call a bull from twenty metres and I do an *estatuario ayudado*, how the public acclaims me! It is theatre, nothing else. That is why the public goes mad, that is why the impresarios pay me more than any other torero today in Spain, and that is why the true experts shake their heads when I fight."

Miguelito's mind contained a canvas and a brush. It painted in the half-dark tavern the rowdy colours of a Sunday afternoon with all seats in sun and shade sold, the crowd leaning forward the better to see its idol, Miguelito. Miguelito slowly advances towards the bull who is about twenty metres away. "Ee-ee-eeh," calls Miguelito, and the bull charges because bulls go where he wants them to go. Feet are together, the two hands lift the *muleta*, the bull sweeps past, with the horns at a few inches from Miguelito's body, the hands open for the *muleta* to canopy the bull, but by then the deadly horns have passed his body.

"Theatre," repeated Miguelito, "but now that it is all over there is one thing I can say to you: I never played the blood act. I pull my belly in like all the others when I call the bull with the *muleta*, but when the horns have passed me I don't stick out my belly as so many others do in order to get it smeared with blood. I fought my bulls close enough. I didn't need the blood of the lance and the *banderillas*. That is all I can say in my favour."

Manolo considered himself a man of ruses. In his opinion he had made Miguelito, though he was the first to admit that it hadn't been difficult to make him. There was talent, brains, guts, a thorough knowledge of bulls and infinite grace. As a man of ruses Manolo turned a deaf ear on the past tense. Probably Miguelito was depressed, so let him say whatever he felt like. Two men entered the tavern, they nudged each other, winked at the barman who winked back at them, and lost in awe and admiration of the great matador, they sat down shaking their heads at the luck that had come their way.

"In your favour," said Manolo. "You speak like a girl of good family. What about your work with the cape? Who today in Spain can make a *veronica* as gracefully as you? Or a *farol*? And your killing? Who kills better than you?"

Manolo blew air through his mouth filled with gold teeth, then sucked the air in.

"Somebody else will have to," said Miguelito quietly. "Manolo, I am through. I called you here to tell you that you're no longer my manager and I am no longer the torero you manage. I have, figuratively, yet in dead earnest, thrown into the Guadalquivir my hat, sword, cape and *muleta*. I am running away from the bulls because I am afraid of them."

"Cachondeo," said Manolo, letting out the air, and "cachondeo" often means a bad practical joke. He laughed to reassure himself. "How can you make such a childish joke? You running from the bulls? There is nobody in the entire world who dominates a bull as you do, there is nobody, not even in the moon, who understands a bull as you do. Man, they talk to you."

"They tell me," said Miguelito, handsome and dignified, "one of them will kill me. I know that because I know them. If you call me a coward I will agree with you, nevertheless I am quitting. I don't want to die like Manolete even if a liqueur is called after me. A fat lot of good the Anis Manolete does him, what?" He laughed to fill in Manolo's silence.

"I don't want to die like Joselito or Manolete, even if I become a national hero. I received the *alternativa* seven years ago when I was twenty one, and I was already a *novillero* when I was eighteen. Ten years of it has killed my nerves." He was speaking quietly, almost speculatively. "I wasn't a flash in the pan, I didn't fight to make money. You know I have far more money than I need. I fought on. Why? Because the great Spanish public wants my skin. That's all I can give it. If I don't die in the ring then I shall disappoint my public. I tell you I won't die. I don't want to please the public any more. I've given it enough : I won't give it my life. And I don't want to please the bulls either. Manolo, I am afraid of bulls, now. I am even afraid of a calf."

"You wouldn't speak like that if your mother were still alive," said Manolo in a woebegone voice, looking funereally down on the dirty marble-top of the table.

Miguelito's mother died two years ago. She was a simple Andalusian woman with vast dimensions, a moustache and varicose veins. Miguelito was born after she'd had seven abortions, and after Miguelito there was no other child, and soon the father died. The mother took her son's success in and without her stride. Somehow it meant nothing to her. She was from the land, her husband had looked after bulls on a bull ranch, and bulls were part and parcel of her existence. It was good and fine that her son excelled but it was of no more importance. He had bought her a house in Puerto de Santa Maria because she was fond of the white town of white wine. In that house she sat the whole day long with women of her age, most of them also moustached. She didn't go to bullfights but prayed during the fights, and after each fight Miguelito dutifully sent her a telegram, and she never listened to the commentaries on the radio. If he came to see her and she trundled at his side in the Calle Larga she didn't observe the curious and admiring glances. He wanted to buy her a motor but she said what good would it do her? She ate a lot of fried fish, then died of heart failure.

"You know my mother doesn't come into this," said

Miguelito. "It meant nothing to her. She was too good and too simple."

"And what will Don Antonio say?" asked Manolo smiling bitterly both for Miguelito and Don Antonio.

Don Antonio was more than a brother could have been to Miguelito, who was born on the estate of Antonio's father—where his own father rode behind bulls and his mother had been a servant girl till her marriage. Antonio's mother was English, which in Lower Andalusia is no rare occurrence. She was pale and fair and couldn't understand why her husband after the initial passion preferred merry-making in Seville to the respectable pleasures of the conjugal bed. She was a dutiful wife but succeeded in giving him only four daughters and one son, which in the husband's eyes didn't amount to much. Antonio was like his father: already at an early age it became evident that his life would consist of shooting, riding, drinking, singing, clapping hands and, of course, women.

"Who would believe that the Englishwoman could have given birth to such a flamenco son?" said those who knew them or heard of Antonio.

What with her husband, insipid snobbish daughters who remained unmarried because nobody was good enough for them, and the too manly son, the Englishwoman began to wilt like a rose in the English summer; till one day her late maid, Miguelito's mother, came to see her on some errand, dragging Miguelito at her side. Antonio's mother immediately felt the boy's gentleness, and became fond of him. While her own son roared round the countryside on his thoroughbreds, or drove his father's Cartuja horses into Jerez, the lonely mother taught Miguelito English and read *In Memoriam* and Rupert Brooke to him. She was still alive when Miguelito

was given the *alternativa* and on that day he offered his
second bull to her. While the newspapers hailed a new
genius of the ring, she, poor soul, cried, for she had
expected better things from her favourite. Now she was
dead five years.

"What indeed will Don Antonio say?" said Manolo
again. "He made you, didn't he? He helped you at the
start, didn't he? Go and tell him you're running from
the bulls."

"I will," said Miguelito. He thought for a while. "I
dream too much of bulls. Every night it is bulls, bulls
and bulls. Manolo, man, the other night in my dream I
killed a Miura bull, and as he dropped I saw two horns
sticking out of my chest. A bull, you see, had come up
from behind, and gored me. Then I saw the ring was full
of bulls, and I, with the horns sticking out of my chest,
ran and jumped the *barrera*, tried to get behind the
burladero; but three bulls were behind it with no room
for me. I gave up and woke up. Now I give up and hope
to wake up."

They were sitting near the door, and a funeral proces-
sion meandered by, the mourners chatting and laughing.
The two men stood up. When they sat down Manolo
said: "Don't talk to me of dreams. I don't like them. We
are now talking of reality." He shouted for two finos.

"Bring a bottle," said Miguelito. "Let me be the
drunken matador for once in my life." When the bottle
was brought he forgot it. "Let us forget dreams," he said.
"I know I am as good as any torero fighting today. I
don't say that to brag because it has nothing to do with
me: it is a gift. Surely during the many times we've been
to Madrid you found time to go to the Prado?"

"I only found time to be present when the lots of bulls

were drawn and to quarrel with the impresario and to be sweet to the journalists."

"Now you'll have time," said Miguelito, "so go to the Prado. Those men who painted the pictures which hang in the Prado had a similar gift: not for bulls but for the art of painting."

"I am sure they didn't risk their lives when they painted," said Manolo.

"Perhaps they risked something else: one never knows. When I was only a boy I already knew bulls. How many times in the callejón did I listen to the peons, even to the mozo de espada giving advice to the matador. 'Work him from the left', 'Turn him round', 'Bring him into the sombra', 'Look out: he pulls to the right'. You never heard my quadrilla giving me advice. At the moment the bull comes in, almost before the first flip of the cape, I know what he is like and I know what to do. I have it here." He tapped his chest, then his forehead. "And here. But it is over. Because I know them, I know one of them will get me. A torero should never think of death. When you fly you shouldn't think of the aeroplane crashing, though there is the possibility. I don't know what other toreros feel like but now I only feel death." He shook his head, slowly, as though astonished by his own words and sentiments. "Are you a believer, have you faith?"

"I?" said Manolo in an indignant voice. "How can you ask me such a question? I am Católico, Apostólico, Romano. Isn't that good enough for you?"

"Sorry, Manolo," said Miguelito. "What I mean is, I won't have to pray so feverishly, so egotistically in the chapel of the Plazas de Toros any more. I will be able to pray for others, not only for my skin."

"The mystic matador," said Manolo and spat more out of habit than disgust.

"I will, for instance, have time to pray for Antonio's mother. You know the poor thing died a Protestant."

"Don't I know that?" said Manolo with true Andalusian lack of reverence for the dead. "Whenever you fought in Cadiz you dragged me to her grave in the British Cemetery at Segunda Aguada. One couldn't even understand what's written on the grave." He wanted to laugh but the seriousness of the situation stifled it. "Are you in earnest or is it, after all, a cachondeo?"

"I am in dead earnest," said Miguelito. "I wouldn't joke with you," and he patted Manolo's shoulder.

"I knew it was coming," said Manolo trying to convince himself that he knew it was coming. "If you quit what will become of me?"

"You are rich enough. Find another Miguelito."

"There isn't one," said Manolo willing to cry. Instead he emptied his glass. "And your quadrilla? Think of José, your peon de confianza."

"Or of Paco, the mozo de espada," said Miguelito, imitating Manolo's reproachful voice. "It won't do. Every one of you will get a big enough money present, more money than you would have earned with me in a year."

"So there won't be even Mexico this winter?" asked Manolo, who had well understood already that there would be no Mexico in the coming winter. As Miguelito shook his head Manolo wanted to shed a few tears but his beady bulging eyes remained as dry as the flat fields round Seville which hadn't seen rain since the spring. He wished he could explain to Miguelito that money as such didn't matter to him, nor to the peons, nor to Paco, and he was certain the picadors themselves would back him up if he found the right words to make Miguelito understand that with his abdication, as it were, a fine and noble association and friendship among several men would collapse. He was moved, and the words didn't come. Then his natural slyness returned.

"We shall see," he said with a huge grin, "what Lolita will have to say."

"I am going to see her now," said Miguelito.

"You'll have fun there. But are you aware of the future in store for you? You won't be able to walk in the streets of Seville, Granada, Malaga and every other town of Andalusia and probably of the whole of Spain, without getting raspberries wherever you go. They will shout after you, you have no cojones, you have no guts, they . . ."

"They won't," said Miguelito rising. "I am leaving Spain. I am going. I am a refugee from the bulls and from myself. All I want you to do is not to let the Press know till I am gone. I am going tomorrow."

"Where are you going?" asked Manolo in a frightened voice; for with Miguelito in some foreign country he couldn't use his influence, couldn't nag him into changing his mind, couldn't persuade him he was behaving foolishly. Going abroad seemed to Manolo as final as being taken to the cemetery.

"To England," said Miguelito.

"Because Antonio's mother taught you English?"

"No; because there is in England something called R.S.P.C.A. and that makes it impossible for anybody to stage a bullfight. I will be under its protection, so to speak, and one day, Manolo, I'll explain what those letters mean. Come, we'll take a taxi and you can drop me at Lolita's house."

"Look, oh look," said Manolo at the door, letting go of Miguelito's arm. On the wall behind them hung a poster announcing a bullfight of the gone summer. The matador on the poster was doing a *natural*, the muleta before the angry yet surprised bull, the matador's right hand almost ready to throw away the sword. Under the picture came the names of two famous matadors, and under their names in twice as large letters the name MIGUELITO. "Look," mumbled Manolo, burst into tears and the two men embraced.

CHAPTER TWO

LOLITA LIVED in the beflowered Barrio de Santa Cruz. She lived in a house next door to a marquesa, and twice she and the marquesa were fined for using foul language in the course of house-to-house arguments. Lolita, having started her career in a brothel, had a fine variety of dirty words at her command, but the marquesa didn't lag behind since she had begun as the late marques's cook. At the present time both women lived in uneasy peace, each acknowledging the other's proficiency. The verbal fight, however, continued among their respective servants, in which Lolita took more interest than the marquesa; for Lolita's maid was her own sister.

Lolita was distinctly good-looking and very desirable to southern eyes. She had everything an Andalusian could wish for : large black eyes, a white skin, dyed fair hair with black streaks near the parting, little or no waist, small breasts, big belly and a huge behind. The legs and arms were thin. She was physically the embodiment of the voluptuous way of life—though not mentally. She cared little for the matters her body was made for; she was interested in uncommonly few things. She could sit still for hours, leaning forward with legs sprawling, and every half hour or so would pat her hair, or touch the lobes of her ears. True she cared for jewels and scent : she cared nothing for success and glory. On the other hand her pride was immense. She looked for offence and usually found it. When she found it hell was let loose. She also had the double gift of not forgetting and not forgiving. She was still prepared, even if it involved five years, to do the marquesa the dirty.

"I don't mind people calling me a whore," she would explain to her sister the maid. "I started as a whore and that for a poor girl is nothing to be ashamed of. But I won't let a cook call me a *puta*."

Her sister agreed. Lolita took life in her stride. Nothing surprised her, and when luck came her way she took it for granted and made no effort to be grateful for it. From the brothel she had moved to a shady night-club where Miguelito eventually picked her up. He fell for her body, and made her his mistress because he could move neither her mind nor her body. To be the mistress of the greatest matador of her time became for her acceptable, hence normal and as it should be. In his almost lacelike shyness Miguelito never let her spread his *capa de paseo* before her at the fights. Though she had her ticket for the barrera she often didn't bother to go at all. She seldom accompanied him in his travels from bull-ring to bullring. Once when Miguelito was badly tossed by a bull and lay motionless in the sand many eyes were on Lolita, who continued quietly to chew her fan. Of ambition she had none. Her sister often urged her to persuade Miguelito to marry her.

"Why should he?" Lolita would answer. "He is far more educated than I."

But she was possessive and diabolically jealous, and that was precisely why on second thoughts Miguelito brought Manolo with him. Lolita was in a good mood and was singing in the drawing-room. She could sing for hours, her mind more vacant than usual but her ears listening entranced to the words of the song. The drawing-room was a garish affair, filled, however, with plants and flowers. Lolita was religiously devoted to plants and flowers, and if a pot were upset her fury was boundless.

"Doce cascabeles tiene mi caballo," she sang, "por la carretera," and her sister let in Miguelito and Manolo. Instead of welcoming them her singing voice rose. The "twelve bells of her horse" filled not so much the road as the room.

"Stop it," said Miguelito. "I want to talk to you." She sang louder. "Didn't you hear me, woman?" he said though he knew it was useless. She sat with her legs wide apart. She never crossed her legs because she believed that wasn't ladylike. Suddenly she stopped singing and burst into laughter. She was as good at laughing as at singing.

"Stop laughing," said Miguelito. "I must talk to you on an important matter." She laughed in his face, then stopped laughing: she had become a trifle curious.

"What is so important?" she asked, then began to hum.

"I have given up the corrida," said Miguelito. "I am through with being a matador."

"That isn't quite so," said Manolo quickly. "The matador is going to travel round the world for the next six months. Nothing less and nothing more, but there is no question of retirement. That's what I am handing out tomorrow to the Press. Nothing final. If you allow me I'll do it right now."

He wasn't loath to go into the next room leaving them alone, and first he telephoned the *ABC*'s Seville office, then *Ya* in Madrid and *El Ruedo*, the bull-fighters' weekly; then he listened to the voices on the other side of the half-open door.

"Chiquillo, I don't understand a single word you say," said Lolita's voice.

"You know I hate being called chiquillo," said Miguelito.

Chiquillo, that is "dear little boy," means in the long run the man is a fool, can't be trusted alone and it is, whether she likes it or not, the woman's duty to look after him, in fine to rule him and to take decisions for him.

"But you are my chiquillo," said Lolita laughing. "Now explain what those mad words mean. One word is madder than the other."

"I am through, I am going," said Miguelito in a tired voice. "It's so simple, can't you understand me?"

"Una mañana," sang Lolita, "de mi Andalucia

Mi puta suegra se quiso casar . . ."

"Shut up," shouted Miguelito, and Lolita hooted with laughter.

"How funny you look, chiquillo, when you're angry," she said.

Manolo thought it was time to rejoin them. Miguelito was standing before Lolita, who still sprawled on the chair, her hands in her wide lap, her body shaking with mirth, mirth which in a sense had nothing to do with the situation.

"Answer me," said Miguelito. "Are you or aren't you coming with me to London?"

"I can't speak French," said Lolita.

"They don't speak French there," said Miguelito. "They speak English."

"London," said Lolita in a dreamy voice, "I saw London. There are many, many flats in London."

"You saw London?" asked Manolo. "Where? In your dreams or in your cups?"

"Don't be rude, you old hog," said Lolita laughing. "I saw London in the cinema. It was a very good film." She leaned forward and Manolo couldn't resist looking down her neck. "Yes, London," she went on. "In that film there was a man and he wanted to marry a girl, and the girl wanted to marry him too, but he said, first, you know, she must see the world, and then—you understand me, chiquillo?—one could see London with many, many flats and buses like those of Madrid, and then the man said here it is, this is London."

It had been an effort and she lapsed into momentary silence.

"Are you or aren't you coming?" asked Miguelito. "Yes or no?"

"No," she said promptly. "I am not going, and you don't go either. If you don't want to fight any more, then don't fight. If you think the bulls will kill you, then keep away from them. Bulls aren't everywhere." She laughed. "I never saw a bull in a tram in my life."

"Bulls are everywhere," said Miguelito and sighed.

"You do exaggerate," said Lolita adopting a motherly attitude, an attitude that had brought her big tips in her earlier life when she helped drunks to undress themselves. "Move into my house for the time being and your Lolita will keep the bulls away."

She laughed so loud that her sister, the maid, came in to see what joke was afoot. "Matilde," said Lolita, between guffaws, "the matador thinks there is a bull under the bed. Go and see. If there is one, chase him out." She looked up. "Where is he?" she asked.

"He's had enough," said Manolo. "He's gone. I'd have gone before."

"You?" said Lolita contemptuously. "You can never keep your eyes off me. Now why did he go?" She went slowly on to the balcony covered with plants and looked down, with Manolo contentedly watching her behind. To look at her body was no treachery to Miguelito : it was part of the routine of his eyes. "I can't see him," she said, coming back into the room. "Do you think he is really going to London?"

"He is," said Manolo flatly.

"He'll soon be back," she said with equanimity. "He loves me too much. He will miss me more than I'll miss him. In fact I never miss anybody. Whenever you went to Mexico I stayed behind, and he always came running back. He'll do the same now."

"I wonder."

"You are heavy," she said. "Don Manolo, you have bored me long enough. I am going with Matilde to the cinema."

As Manolo went down the stairs he heard her singing :

Echame niño bonito
Lágrimas en un pañuelo
Y me llevaré a Granada
Que las engarce un platero.

CHAPTER THREE

MIGUELITO RODE in a taxi to Antonio's estate.
Though he could have owned a string of Rolls-Royces, Miguelito had no motor; on the other
hand he was devoted to taxis, taxis at all times,
taxis to whatever distant place he wished to go;
and it would happen that in Huelva, for instance,
he would hail a cab and tell the astounded driver
in a quiet voice to take him to Barcelona. He sat
well back in the yellow taxi thinking of Lolita. Part of
him would have preferred to take her warm body to
unknown London, a town he was assured was eternally
covered in fog. Her laughter might have cut through the
fog. But another part of him was glad she understood
nothing and therefore wouldn't accompany him; for she
belonged to the life from which he was cutting himself
off. She might, he thought in sudden fright, bring the
spirit of the bulls and the ring with her. On a night of
panic witnessed only by bed and four walls he had made
his mind up. The panic wasn't caused by the sheer
physical fear of the horns : it was caused by his own love
of them. He shook his head because he couldn't even
explain it to himself. He saw himself as a refugee, a
fugitive, and thanked Our Lady of the Miracles that he
would be irrevocably away tomorrow. The matador, said
the driver to himself, as he caught a glimpse of him in
the driving glass, looks sad and so young, and you

wouldn't believe he is the same man you see in the ring.
The shrunken giant; and those two words pleased the
driver.

The taxi passed the spiked wires behind which peace-
fully grazed Antonio's fighting bulls. Miguelito couldn't
resist looking at them. The brown one over there has
good horns and good weight. I like that black one with
the white patch under the left eye. I could do with him
whatever I wanted. Now the one on the left, I am sure,
will be a *manso* in the ring. He sat up with a jerk. He
mustn't look at them, he mustn't think of them, and the
taxi stopped before the house.

Antonio wasn't yet back to luncheon though it was six
in the evening. So said his wife without resignation but
out of sheer habit, since Antonio frequently came to lunch
at seven in the evening, or skipping the meal would turn
up in the middle of the night. They had been married
for four years, had four children, and the wife was
pregnant with the fifth. Antonio's proud, unmarried
sisters were in the house, and it amused Miguelito to
chat with them. They spoke condescendingly to him
because his mother had once been a servant in the house;
they also spoke coyly to him, and all four of them would
have been delighted to marry the famous matador. Now
and then he wouldn't have minded finding out what
those proud spinsters might be like in bed. Ashamed of
himself he would dismiss them from his thoughts. Accord-
ing to his code one shouldn't harbour such fantasies
about the sisters of the man who was more than a
brother. He sat with them and with Maria, the wife,
half listening to their women's tittle-tattle, half counting
the minutes and the hours separating him from the
Seville-London aeroplane. At eight o'clock Antonio

arrived in his Buick. He was a large man, who was trying to show with each moment that he was the embodiment of his own ideal personality, the *caballero Andaluz*. Every movement was also a protest against his English blood.

"Have you eaten?" asked his wife.

"I had some *tapas* in Seville," he said. "I don't feel hungry. Where are the children?" His wife collected the children, he kissed them, then drank a glass of sherry. He was standing like a stranger, like one who had practically no contact with the house. "What brings you here?" he asked Miguelito, putting his arm round his shoulder.

"He is off tomorrow to London," said one of the sisters.

Antonio frowned. "London?" he said as though he hadn't heard of that town before. "London? Are you off your head?"

"I think I am," said Miguelito.

"It's no good talking here," said Antonio, looking at his wife, sisters and children; "come into my office." And he took him to the room his mother had always referred to as the study. The walls were covered with photographs of bulls, toreros and fights, including one of Miguelito doing a *quite*. They sat down facing each other at the desk and Antonio poured out wine which Miguelito didn't touch. He spoke for nearly half an hour and Antonio didn't interrupt. When he had finished there was silence for a few minutes with Antonio masterfully holding the stem of his glass. Then he took his hand off it.

"I understand you," he said. "It has become too much for you. You see, you are an artist with a conscience. You always give everything. You aren't like so many others who say: no, not at this corrida, it isn't worth while; and they pocket the money, give the public nothing and take no risks. You who know bulls as well as they do, you always took risks, you risked your life whenever you went into the ring."

"Till lately it didn't occur to me I was risking my life," said Miguelito, looking at his own photograph. "It wasn't risky for me because, for instance, I would say to myself: now this one I've got to punish with the *capa* till I get the *bicho* to do what I want, or I'd say to the bull, I'll give you ten *pases por alto* if necessary but you do the *natural* with me as I want it." He pointed at the photograph. "Do you remember that bull? He wouldn't go near the horse, he was just backing away from it, and found a *querencia* and there he stood ploughing up the sand, and I went up to him with the capa and said, come, and I ran before him with the capa before me, he behind me as if afraid to lose me, and then I just waved the capa and he went straight into the horse. That is how it was but it can't be like that any more. It's gone, Antonio. If I were ordered to fight tomorrow, I think I would die in my sleep. My nerves and heart would give up if they knew there was a fight tomorrow."

Miguelito bowed his head and Antonio leaned over the desk putting both arms round his neck. Miguelito shook with swallowed sobs; for he had been afraid of Antonio, afraid Antonio would laugh at him.

"Perhaps I haven't the right to feel like that," said Miguelito.

"Only a great artist has the right to feel like that."

"But if I feel like that I have ceased to be a great artist."

"You were long enough a great artist," said Antonio,

and being half English and therefore more preoccupied with the morrow than he should have liked to admit, he asked, "What will you do in London?"

Miguelito thought for a few seconds before he answered. "I don't really know," he admitted. "I said London because in England there are no *toros bravos* and because, so an Englishman once explained to me, the government would fall if a corrida were allowed. That's good enough for me. You have been to London, what is London like?"

"Awful," said Antonio promptly, "but there is one great redeeming thing there. Women go to bed with you."

"You mean the prostitutes?"

"No, decent women."

"But if they go to bed with a man who isn't their husband then they are *putas*."

"Miguelito," said Antonio laughing, "if you want to be in London you must forget the outlook of our beautiful and honest Andalusia. Of women you'll have plenty, and there is one thing I want to warn you about : don't go to the big hotels. There will be other Spaniards and you will be recognised, and then you might just as well come back. If you want to be alone and alone, then just disappear in London : it's big enough. I could give you letters to my awful English cousins but then it would be the same thing again."

"How well you understand me," said Miguelito.

"And now," said Antonio, "we'll spend your last night here together. We will go into Seville and in the morning I'll see you off."

"Can I write some letters first?"

"Of course," said Antonio and left him, on which

Miguelito moved into his seat and wrote first to Luis, his peón de confianza.

"My dear Luis," the letter said, "how will I be able to explain it to you? I am leaving the bulls and the ring, I am leaving all the glory in which you were of such great help to me. I am leaving everything and everybody because that is the only thing I can do. I am going without seeing you, without embracing you. Part of me is ashamed to leave you and let you down, but another part of me, the part which rules me now, is glad, relieved and will take me to London which means I shall be gone for good from you. That side of me you and the others of my beloved quadrilla won't want to see, the other side would just break down if I went to say goodbye, and then there probably would be no goodbye. I am sending you a cheque which you are to divide up with Juan and Pepe. There is a cheque here for Bartolo and Joaquin the picadors, and tell Joaquin not to get too drunk with the money. This is roughly what you'd have earned if we had gone to Mexico this coming winter. Go with God my beloved friends and forgive me, but my mind is made up because my frightened heart says so."

He signed the letter, wiped off a tear, then calculated again and wrote out the cheque. There was one more letter to write—a more difficult letter. It was for Paco, the mozo de espada.

"Paco," he wrote, "you will never dress me any more." That was frighteningly final. "You will never stand in the callejón waiting with the swords for me, your dear, faithful eyes not leaving me for a second. You are too young to understand what I myself still hardly understand. If you want to forget me for having let you down, I can't stop you, and now I will say no more. I know you are the best mozo de espada, so you won't have difficulty in finding employment and this cheque will give you the time you need to do nothing for a long time, but don't give any money to your father; he will drink it which isn't good for him."

As there was so much more he wanted to say to Paco, he signed the letter, and went next door, that is into the drawing-room. Antonio's mother had covered the room in chintz which had faded under the Andalusian sun, and what with lack of interest and care it had become a sad room; but neither Antonio nor his wife worried about that.

"What's happened?" asked Maria. "You look ill."

"It's nothing," said Miguelito, and took a drink from Antonio. Many drinks tonight, he thought: the only way out.

The sisters asked him whether he would remain in London for long. He said he hoped all his life, which made Antonio remark it was foolish to discuss the day after tomorrow; for tomorrow was more than enough. Antonio said it was time for them to leave, so Miguelito shook hands all round, kissed the children and Maria resignedly escorted the two men to the motor. She was resigned because she knew that with Miguelito going her husband would go on a bout of at least three days. If only, she thought without finding words for her thought, men could give women the love and consideration they give one another.

"Look," said Antonio as they drove past the grazing bulls, "that one there will be a beauty."

"I won't look," said Miguelito, taking in the bull. Yes, he was a beauty.

"Shall we start in a brothel?" asked Antonio.

"Not yet," said Miguelito, "and I won't go to Lolita either. I leave her with the bulls."

Antonio laughed and because he saw his point Miguelito laughed too. They stopped in Seville at a café to which Manolo went every evening at eight o'clock. They found him quiet and depressed, drank with him, were joined by a man resembling a jockey who has taken to fat. He was a famous Andalusian breeder of bulls.

"Don Jesús," shouted Antonio, "this will be our night, the night of the four of us."

It was. The night for Miguelito was akin to a rainbow with him darting from sun to rain and from rain to sun. At times the hues were brighter; now and then they only winked at him. They dined in the restaurant next door to the bus station; after dinner they drank bottles of brandy; after the brandy they were in some large room where a gipsy boy and a gipsy girl danced for them; and people drifted in from the street or perhaps dropped from the ceiling. Hands clapped, the gipsy called the girl with his hands and feet as a torero should call a bull; a fat man whom nobody knew sang in the corner and among roars of laughter had a fight with the guitarist. A strange orchestra with trumpets and one saxophone drifted in from the street, and was thrown out. There was conversation too.

"Miguelito," said Don Jesús, "the trouble with you as with all modern toreros is that you won't admit the bull is the centre of the lidia. You want to make yourselves the centre. But it is the bull. You are almost worse than the others because you react too much to the public. There are bulls which must be punished by the lance of the picador or he'll be no good for the work with the muleta. But you want applause. I have seen you a hundred times, so I know what I am talking about. The picador stabs the bull, the ignorant public shrieks and whistles, and you, instead of ignoring it, turn to the presidency and ask for the picadors to go, and that of course suits the public, and so you are the public's darling, and you remain with a bull who would have been fifty times better if more punished. Miguelito, the bull comes before the torero. It is he who matters most."

"Then why," asked Miguelito, "isn't the bull allowed to cut the torero's ear?" He thought that funny and original, and stopped laughing only when he saw that nobody was laughing with him. "Anyway," he said, "don't talk of bulls to me, Don Jesús. I am sick of them." It was the turn of Don Jesús to laugh. The great Miguelito sick of bulls, and his laughter almost drowned the clapping and the guitar.

Now the gipsy girl came up and sat down at Miguelito's feet. She smelt strongly of cheap eau-de-Cologne. "Matador," she said, "you are the handsomest man I've ever seen." He pulled away the hand she had taken, for he was thinking of Lolita, whom his drink-sodden body wanted badly. But Lolita would laugh, he would lie down beside her and there would be no aeroplane to London. The gipsy girl went to dance again.

"Manolo," said Miguelito, "if she needs anything let her have it. I'll give it back to you."

"She needs nothing," said Manolo. "You bought her the house, she has money in the bank, she has more than she wants."

"I am sick of all this," shouted Antonio. "Get out, all of you." He threw a thousand pesetas note to the gipsies. "And enough of this horrible noise. Come on, we're going to a café. It is six o'clock already. Only two hours left, Miguelito."

On their way to the nearest café they lost Don Jesús, the rainbow also went and there was only the dawn in the street with a few workmen in the café drinking coffee and talking in low voices as befits men who are still sleepy. Manolo was in tears.

"I think I will give you the address of my English cousins," said Antonio. "You will be very lonely away from us and your glory. I don't think they'll cheer you up but at least you'll know there are people you can go and see. One of them, Jane, will make you laugh. She is much taller than you, there is nothing of the woman about her, and I can assure you you'll just stare and laugh at her. She breeds dogs, that's all she is good for."

"What are the English really like?" asked Miguelito. "You've been there, you ought to know."

"They have no sense of humour," said Antonio who was drinking white wine again, "so don't joke with them. They don't understand a cachondeo. If you tell an Englishman you're eighty years old he'll believe you and say you look young for your years, and to reassure you will tell you he knew a man who lived to be a hundred. And they are all afraid of death, yet they all think of tomorrow and the day after."

"Manolo," said Miguelito in a pitiful voice, "telephone the Andalusia Palace to send somebody with my luggage to the airport."

"Miguelito," said Manolo, "hasn't the joke lasted long enough?"

"It isn't a joke : go and telephone, please."

What with chatting about the English and swallowing more wine, Antonio forgot to give him his cousins' address. When they embraced and said goodbye at the aerodrome Antonio repeated the English had no sense of humour.

3—SS

"They could never understand your big joke," he added.

"What big joke?" asked Miguelito.

"Your joke about giving up bullfighting."

"But it isn't a joke," shouted Miguelito and was told to get into the aeroplane.

CHAPTER FOUR

MIGUELITO, WHO had left his luggage at Waterloo, crossed Waterloo Bridge, looking at the river. There was room in that river both for the Guadalete and the Guadalquivir. Too much water, and how dirty and turbulent, he said to himself. Then, without saying by your leave, a voice in his mind asked whether Don Jesús was right when he said he minded the public's reaction above his knowledge. He stopped. If he started to think of Don Jesús, of the lidia, of the bulls . . . his thoughts were cut short; for it was already the rush hour and those who rushed nearly tripped him over. Having reached the other side of the bridge, he saw a street with many red buses, that is the Strand, and tried to get there, but it was hard work with the pushing crowd. This, he admitted, wasn't the town for him, and his lithe body had to fight its slender way through a crowd bigger than at a bullfight. Instinct drove him into a quieter street on the other side of the Strand. He found a public house and went in. He would have been surprised to learn that the pub was still closed half an hour ago. He looked at the bottles and saw a bottle labelled Tio Pepe. That cheered him up, making him feel a little less a bewildered stranger.

"One glass of Tio Pepe," he said to the barmaid, a blowsy blonde of forty summers. He spoke English as though it were a dead language, and a memorial at the same time to Antonio's mother.

"What?" asked the barmaid.

"One glass of Tio Pepe white wine," said Miguelito.

"You mean sherry," she said and turned to her colleague, another blowsy blonde of forty summers. "These foreigners do talk funny." She gave him the drink, which Miguelito necked down, and as he was going to ask for another, she said: "One and ninepence."

"I beg your pardon," said Miguelito.

"It's one and ninepence," she said holding out her hand. "You understand? One and ninepence."

"I will pay when I go," said Miguelito. "I want one more glass."

"You pay your way in this country," said the other barmaid. "You get a drink, pay for it, then if you want another, ask for it, then pay for it."

"Come on, sir, I'm in a 'urry," said the first barmaid and they both glared at Miguelito, who was now smiling, thinking of Antonio's words. He was right: the English had no sense of humour. Miguelito pulled out a five pound note. "'Aven't the change for it," said the barmaid.

"I beg your pardon," said Miguelito. "I don't understand you well."

"What a bore this foreigner is," said the first barmaid to her public. "You give me small money, get me? One and ninepence. Small money, like this." She held up a half-crown. "See? Money like this."

The licensee, a fat fellow with an ash-covered waistcoat, came on to the scene.

"I have no small money like that," said Miguelito, whose Andalusian soul was beginning to enjoy itself. "But I give you this big money, you keep it and when I drink you," he searched for the word, "deduct. I have confidence in you."

In the silence that followed you could hear the swishing of a Spanish angel's wings.

"I am afraid, sir," said the licensee, "you misunderstood Rosy. What she meant was that here in this country one pays when the drink is served. I understand you completely. I know Continental habits: I've been to France." Which was true. He had once gone on a passportless day-excursion to Rouen, where he lunched on the boat afraid of the muck they serve on the Continent. "I know you gentlemen there pay when you leave. It isn't so here." He gave his humble hangers-on a triumphant look, implying that nobody else could handle so ticklish a situation as well as he could. "But as regards depositing a five-pound note, I am afraid, sir, it is against the rules of the house. I am the licensee."

Miguelito thought that was his name. Antonio's mother had told him of The Mackintosh and so on. Miguelito held out his hand and said, "How do you do?"

"How do you do, sir?" said the licensee and winked at the hangers-on, men who laid bets through him, men whose financial conscience made them buy him drinks with no reward. "To oblige you, sir, I will take this five-pound note upstairs and make an exception to the rule and change it." He had eighty pounds on him for betting purposes but didn't want the hangers-on to see the contents of his wallet.

"But I want more drink," said Miguelito, and wished Antonio could witness the scene.

"While I go and change this," said the licensee with the fiver in his hand, "have as many drinks as you like, sir. Rosy, serve the gentleman with whatever he fancies."

"I must say I never heard him speak to me like that," said a man beside Miguelito, who had two more drinks of sherry and asked the man next to him to join him.

"A large scotch," said the man promptly, and Rosy gave him a hard look.

"Don't buy him a drink," she said to Miguelito. "He's a scrounger."

Miguelito, having not the faintest idea what the word scrounger meant, bought him a second large scotch, then received his change. The scrounger gave Rosy a wink, and then to his surprise he saw that Miguelito had left. Those damned foreigners, he decided, just lead you up the garden path.

It was raining lightly, which held no surprise for Miguelito. First rain, and fog would soon follow. The English were amusing, and that poor fellow who was so hopeful after his drink, didn't he know that in Spain he had soul-mates by the thousand who hoped as he had for gallons of free drinks? The scrounger had somehow showed Miguelito that he wasn't in an altogether alien land, and his loneliness lifted a little. He went into another bar, where he liked the barmaid's appearance. When she brought his sherry and he held out the money he tried quickly to caress her hand. She gave him a furious glance, then walked away haughty and offended. Miguelito was puzzled. Did Antonio joke saying English women liked that kind of thing? He tried to catch her eye and succeeded, only to see her toss her head and push out her chin.

"These foreigners," she said to a pet customer, who heartily agreed with her.

The pub was more than half empty. A man holding an Alsatian on a lead sat at a table reading the *Evening Standard*. The Alsatian wanted to get at a moth-eaten wire-haired terrier, who growled under a Guinness-drinking old woman's table. The hand holding the leash seemed in agony. At the bar was a man with a red nose, wearing a bowler hat. He was drinking mild and bitter, his eyes focused on Miguelito, who was wearing a dark grey suit and a black tie. He had worn only black ties since Antonio's mother died.

"I take it, sir," said the man in the bowler hat, "you are a foreigner." He took Miguelito's silence for reproof, and added quickly: "There is nothing to be ashamed of if one is a foreigner. We are as God made us." Miguelito began to understand his high-pitched Cockney. "Are you French, sir?"

"I am a Spaniard," said Miguelito.

"A Spaniard? That's very interesting, sir. I used to be a merchant seaman and I've been to Barcelona, to Alicante, to Seville and Cadiz."

"This morning I was still in Seville," said Miguelito and as he said that, the bar, the barmaid, the alien bottles and the Alsatian, too, became incredible, in fact untrue.

"That's a beautiful town," said the seaman. "All them orange trees. I had a lovely time there, and the people was so nice and 'orspitable. All the nonsense they talk 'ere of the Spanish. They say all of them are toreadors and just go about in fancy-dress killing bulls." He tee-heed, showing his National Health Service teeth. "Well, I always say it's just a lot of balls. Am I right in saying there are no more bullfights in Spain? I've read that somewhere."

"No, there still are," sighed Miguelito.

"Well, that's a pity if I may say so. That poor bull, he never gets a chance. All the dice are loaded against him.

They just bring him into the pit or whatever they call it and just stab him to death. Isn't that so?"

"I don't like bulls and I don't like bullfights," said Miguelito looking ironically at his reflection in the glass behind the row of bottles. "So, please, we will speak of something else, yes?"

"I admire your sentiments," said the seaman. "You talk like a man. If all Spaniards were like you, then they would stop butchering them poor animals. I do admire your sentiments. May I ask you to take a drink with me?"

Miguelito accepted and thus ended abruptly his premeditated loneliness. The seaman soon gave him the story of his life. He was called Cook.

"You are a cook?" interjected Miguelito.

"No," teeheed Cook. "My name is Cook : Ted Cook."

He had been a merchant seaman for twenty years and was at present the janitor of a block of flats in Knightsbridge. The block of flats was an expensive affair, some flats cost as much as eight hundred a year. He eyed the Spaniard hoping he would be impressed, but having worked out how many pesetas that was, Miguelito remained unimpressed. In Mexico or in Madrid or in Barcelona he easily paid double that.

"It's only for the very wealthy," said Ted Cook apologetically.

Miguelito nodded and they had another round. Ted Cook held up his sixth mild and bitter. When he emptied it he was ready to speak of his wife. The seventh brought down the frontiers of reticence. His wife, whichever way you looked at her, was a bitch. She nagged and nagged and got drunk on Guinness, but woe to Ted Cook if he came home a little pickled. Because she drank in their basement flat and not in pubs, she considered herself as good as a teetotaler.

"But I," he said, "I'm the drunk because I 'ave my daily pint."

When he had emptied the eighth pint Miguelito asked him whether he knew of a hotel in the neighbourhood, explaining the hotel shouldn't be expensive. Antonio in the course of the previous night had twice impressed on him the need to keep away from the big hotels if he didn't want to be recognised.

"Now that needs a lot of thinking," said Ted Cook. "I don't want you to go to them boarding-houses in Bayswater. That's the Christie country." He teeheed but Miguelito didn't know what the Christie country could be. "I don't want you to go near Paddington either. Too many tarts there."

"Tarts?"

"Prostitutes."

"I see, but are they nice?"

"They ain't nice, you take that from me. Now look here, signore," he said, proud of his acquaintance with foreign languages, "you're 'ere just off Long Acre, so you go to Russell Square, it ain't far, and there you find plenty of cheap 'otels, but be careful of the tarts because they're everywhere these days."

"I must first fetch my luggage," said Miguelito, "won't you, please, come with me and help to find a hotel?"

As Ted Cook said of course he would, Miguelito remembered Manolo's words of the night before, coming, as it were, from under the rainbow. "You," said Manolo, "who have had hangers-on, followers, admirers and self-appointed servants for over ten years, you won't be able to do without them. A man like you can't divest himself any more. You'll pick them up in England or at the end of the earth. Don't look at yourself as the lonely exile. You have lost the gift of being alone." Antonio agreed with him.

"I think I shouldn't molest you by asking to accompany me," Miguelito said.

"It's a pleasure," said Ted Cook. Miguelito bought a bottle of beer for Ted Cook to drink in the cab, which he did remarkably swiftly; they collected the luggage, and the search for a hotel began in and around Russell Square. Ted Cook proved to be a chooser : here he didn't care for the room, there he didn't fancy the price. He argued with unpleasant managers and morose manageresses, who were glad to see the pair go.

"You need something decent," he said, getting into the cab for the tenth time. "One can see you're a gent, a gentleman you know, even if a foreign gentleman."

"My mother was a maid," said Miguelito, "and my father looked after . . ." he decided not to say bulls, "cattles."

"Blimey," said Ted Cook. "I'd 'ave sworn you 'ad blue blood."

Blue blood, thought Miguelito. Perhaps blood turned blue after generations of abject poverty, of true resignation to the will of God, of looking for generations after those noble beasts the toros bravos.

"Oi," shouted Ted Cook to the driver, "stop 'ere. I like the look of it."

It was only after they rang the bell that they caught sight of a notice saying HOTEL FULL. Ted swore, but as they were going to turn away a pink-faced Irishman with ginger hair opened the door.

"Sorry, mate," said Ted. "Didn't see the notice when I rang the bell. It was for this 'ere foreign gentleman."

"That's okay," said the Irishman. "I always put it up when I'm having supper."

"Now that's clever," said Ted admiringly. "Let's see the rooms."

To Miguelito the rooms seemed neither better nor worse than the rooms he had seen before. Ted, however, was enthusiastic and had already taken to the Irishman. The upshot was that Miguelito moved into Number 10 on the second floor. It was a dismal room with faded wallpaper from the days when the house had been a private residence, and the springs of the one armchair were gone. On the other hand in Spanish provincial towns the matador often had to sleep in less comfortable rooms, and besides he was tired of going from hotel to hotel; so he agreed with Ted, and the Irishman brought up his expensive luggage, which only emphasised the sordid look of the room. Ted promised to meet him in the same public house on the following evening.

"And now," he said, "I'd better go back and see if she's locked me out."

Miguelito didn't understand, so he had to explain in detail.

"A woman to lock out a man?" said Miguelito aghast. "That just couldn't exist in Spain. A woman wouldn't dare to do that. A man—the man is the master. I can't believe it."

"There are lots of things here which you wouldn't believe," said the Irishman, to which Ted agreed and went his way.

"I am going out for a walk now," said Miguelito to the Irishman.

"Pubs are already closed," said the Irishman; then, observing that Miguelito was looking at him blankly, he explained the licensing hours. Still, said Miguelito to himself, there was the R.S.P.C.A. at least.

Nevertheless he went for a walk. The rain had been driven away by the east wind which had dried the pavement and made Miguelito shiver a little. He crossed Russell Square and in a little while found himself in Guilford Street.

"Come with me, ducks," hissed a voice, "I'll give you a good time."

The woman stood against the wall, her figure too slim for his liking, her face dominated by the lipstick which tried to enlarge her mouth. She had an undernourished appearance and was a cross between impertinence and servility. He wanted to go on, but it occurred to him that if he went with her he would go to bed with an Englishwoman, which he hadn't done before. You can't know a country without knowing its women. Moreover, he was missing Lolita, and that thin body would be such a contrast.

"Yes, please," he said.

She took him to a room with a distinctly dirty appearance but he had to admit the sheets were almost clean. She had little to say. She asked him if he were a foreigner, and when satisfied she took two pounds from him, then undressed. Her body was as he had expected: the ribs could be counted, the skin was rough, and her nipples were like cherries left behind on the barrow. With his mind full of Lolita he made vehement love to her. She let it be, and when he left, her comment to herself was "Barmy."

A wizened man sold him two boxes of matches and three pairs of shoe-laces on his way back to the hotel. The Irishman let him in and Miguelito went to his room, where he took Lolita's photograph from a suit-case. She was staring straight at the camera, her mouth half open. She had learned that from watching one of her favourite film stars. He sat with the photograph and when he thought he was ready for sleep he got into bed. Then came what in his native land is called a night of Toledo. His dreams were stormy and grey, full of symbols which even the dreamer couldn't fathom. There were moments of sunny brightness with Joaquin the picador nudging his horse forward, then the grey storm swallowed the light. He found himself standing quietly in the *callejón* with the folded cape in his arms, his nostrils smelling the freshly ironed silk; but a wave which had no watery substance lifted him, he shouted to Paco who couldn't hear him, and now he knew that it wasn't a wave : it was a cloud consisting of boos and jeers. The cloud dropped him into the Parque Maria Luisa in Seville. It was November as in London; for the chrysanthemums were everywhere. He was dressed for the corrida and a woman was walking at his side, a woman who wasn't Lolita. He couldn't see her though there was no doubt that she was a woman. He stopped, took off his hat and turned round in a circle holding his hat out.

"I am offering this woman, whom I am going to kill, to you the flowers," he said and threw the hat on a chrysanthemum, which made him wake up.

At least there was no bull in my dream, he said to reassure himself. He put on the light, the room looked dejected as if it were having a night of Toledo too. He drank water but didn't care for it, lay down, was whisked back into the park in Seville, and the woman wasn't there. Probably he had already killed her.

CHAPTER FIVE

"WHAT IS this?" asked Miguelito staring with bloodshot, sleepy eyes at a fried egg, fat bacon, too white bread, margarine and a spoonful of orange marmalade which was congealed. "Please, what is this?"

"Your breakfast," said the Irishman.

"I don't eat this breakfast," said Miguelito. "I can never eat this."

"You should, it's good for you."

"No, thank you very much and please take it away. It will only make me sick, but leave the tea."

"In that case," said the Irishman, "I might eat it myself. They don't feed me too well here. You don't mind?"

"No, no, please sit down and eat."

The Irishman took the tray to the table, sat down and devoured the egg and the bacon while Miguelito drank the strong, dark tea. Someone in the next room started knocking on the wall.

"Don't take any notice of him," said the Irishman. "He's daft. He's a retired schoolmaster from Wales, thinks his family wants to rob him, so lives here, pays every morning with a pound note, then roams the streets the whole day long, and now he is knocking on the wall because he thinks it is still night and doesn't want to be disturbed. I wake him at half past nine and till I go in he thinks it's eleven at night or something." The knocking became furious. "Go easy, Taffy," bellowed the Irishman. "I'll come and wake you in ten minutes."

The British, thought Miguelito, were a strange lot. The Irishman had swallowed bacon, egg, bread, margarine and marmalade, so Miguelito asked him to open the window and let the smell out. Through the open window light sunrays danced into the room.

"You call me Micky," said the Irishman sitting down on the bed. "The fools round here call me Moike because I'm Irish and they all think they can speak Oirish or whatever they call it, but I am Micky to my friends. I bet you don't even notice I speak like an Irishman." Miguelito shook his head. "There you are. I don't notice it myself." The knocking became loud. "That's that bastard. Now he just pretends it's eleven at night, actually he's hungry and wants his breakfast. I'll be back."

Left alone Miguelito went to the window and drank in the sunshine. It was a frail sun that sent out the rays. Miguelito had the impression that if the sun weren't careful the rays would drop into the street before they reached the window. In the street below the window a few people were moving at no brisk pace on their way to bookshops and publishers' offices. His eyes followed a pretty girl till she turned the corner, but, oh, why were these English women like toothpicks? A little later a fat woman waddled by, making Miguelito shake his head. When they were fat they were ungainly. Suddenly he wanted those people in the street to look up at the window, nudge each other and whisper: "There is Miguelito, the great matador." Ashamed of himself he turned away from the window.

The bathroom was on the floor below and on his way down to it he met the schoolmaster on the lower landing. The schoolmaster, who was evidently coming from the bathroom, wore flannel pyjamas with a faded overcoat above them. He was small and podgy, his face was red. As he beheld the red silk cloud that were Miguelito's pyjamas and dressing-gown, his eyes dilated and the now purple skin was ready to burst.

"What is this?" he bellowed. "Is this a male brothel? Mike, come here at once, kick this nancy boy out."

Miguelito, unaware of being the nancy boy, went quietly into the bathroom and locked the door. On the other side of the door the Irishman was trying to soothe the Welshman.

"What you don't understand," the Irishman was saying, "is the big world, and this gentleman, he comes from the big world and not from a Welsh mining village."

"Are you saying I come from a mining village?" asked the schoolmaster in a threatening voice.

"Where else can you come from if you come from Wales?"

"Is that so?" said the schoolmaster. "Well, just let me tell you I come from Montgomeryshire and where I come from there are no mines, and I am a Welshman from the land of Lloyd George, Vaughan Williams and Dylan Thomas, you see? And you're just a bloody Ulsterman, a lackey of the English, but we the Welsh will be one day back in Shropshire, you see?"

"Now, Taffy, if you tell me where Shropshire is, then I'll tell you whether you'll be back there or not. Meantime you'd better go back to your room or people will start complaining about the noise."

The Irishman ran down the stairs, and the Welshman stamped back to his room muttering about Shropshire and male brothels; and Miguelito sat quietly in his bath thinking of Lolita. Later, when he had dressed, he rang for Micky, who came still giggling because of Shropshire.

"I want to ask you, please," said Miguelito, "what I should visit today in London? I am for first time here."

"If I go out visiting," said Micky, "I usually go to Mooney's Irish House but as you aren't 'Oirish,'" he laughed, "go to the British Museum. It's round the corner. All the foreigners go there."

Yes, the British Museum, Doña Mary—she had fought hard not to become Doña Maria—Antonio's mother had frequently spoken of the British Museum to Miguelito, and the longer she lived in Spain the bigger and more wonderful the British Museum became for her. It contained every treasure under the sun and the moon and all the valuable marbles in the world. The very mention of it made Miguelito look solemn.

"Not on the first day of my life in London," he said. "I want to see the centre of the town and the Piccadilly."

"Take the 38 bus and you'll be there in a jiffy for twopence."

Micky had left the door open and now the schoolmaster appeared on the landing ready to start on his peregrinations. He had on the same old overcoat but instead of pyjama legs he wore pepper-and-salt tweed trousers. Micky called to him.

"Taffy," he said, "I've been studying that Shropshire business. Now if I was you I'd take Cheshire first, then you could cut off Shropshire, and from Cheshire you could attack Liverpool. Man, you need a port after all. In every military operation one needs a port."

"I'll think of it," said the schoolmaster gravely, caught sight of the elegant figure with starched collar and black tie and bowed to it, not for a moment connecting it with the nancy boy who had surely escaped from a male brothel. "Yes, I'll think of it. Time is short, the hour-glass is running out. Good morning, gentlemen."

Miguelito warmed to the British. Though he understood hardly anything of the conversation, he guessed that it was an example of a cachondeo, and if a nation knew how to practice cachondeo then it deserved his love. He asked Micky to join him for a drink in the evening in the pub where he was meeting his other new friend: Ted Cook.

"Most of them here have latchkeys," said Micky, "and them as haven't can wait. It won't kill them. I'll come."

In Piccadilly Miguelito bought a bowler hat and an umbrella. The looking-glass told him he looked like any other well-dressed man in the street, which was precisely what he asked from the glass. Fortified by that belief, he walked along Piccadilly in the sunshine, the umbrella hanging on his arm, and women said to themselves, he moves as beautifully as a ballet-dancer. When he reached Hyde Park Corner he stopped, and saw that London, so notorious abroad for its fog, was a white town. He had seen many white towns in Spain and North Africa, but this was a different kind of white. It had no glare, it didn't hurt the eye: that whiteness belonged to the frail sun in the light blue sky. He stood and stared and the whiteness seeped into him. After a long while he turned round and retraced his steps. He wanted to see that famous yet so disappointingly small Piccadilly Circus again. As he walked past Green Park Station, content in himself, an escapee from a night of Toledo, a voice behind him with a very strong English accent said: "Matador." Miguelito's ears began to burn and his pace quickened. "Matador, please matador, oiga, stop for a moment." Miguelito decided to run for it, but his follower had decided on it earlier. He sprinted past him, then faced him. They were already under the Ritz arcades. The pursuer was a tall, hatless young man with a carefully arranged lock falling to his right eyebrow. He had a long nose and flashy wet lips. He had a slight stoop too. During his stroll Miguelito had noticed young men who looked very similar.

"Oh do forgive me, great maestro," wailed the young man, "but I spotted you at once at Hyde Park Corner. You see, I am such an aficionado. I have been to twelve corridas. I am writing a book about the fiesta brava. I saw you fight seven times, seven out of twelve, not bad, what? I saw you twice in the Monumental in Madrid, saw you in Pamplona, in Valencia, in Murcia, also in Cáceres. So you see I am not a complete stranger. Oh do forgive me, great Miguelito."

"You think I am somebody else, please," said Miguelito.

"No and no, there is only one Miguelito in the world. You are my captive, maestro. You must come and have a drink with me here in the Ritz. This has made my day. You don't know what this means to me. My name is John Chaytor."

"If my name is Miguelito," said Miguelito, hoping Manolo couldn't hear it from the distance, "then you should must know I am retired from the fighting for good and always."

"What does it matter after the rapture you have given us? May I take your arm and shepherd you to a drink. I do love the Spanish custom of men walking arm in arm, or with hands on each other's shoulders. Here the barbarians snigger at it." He took Miguelito's arm. "On second thoughts," he said, "why waste a fortune on drinks in the Ritz? Come, matador, we'll go to a little, typically English pub and have a drink there."

"Yes, please," said Miguelito, smiling at the thought that the drinking public knew no frontiers. Let's have a drink in the Palace but if I come to think of it why not go to the tavern at the corner? "Wherever you wish, but, please, don't call me matador. I am retired. Call me Mr. Perez, that is my real, common name. Very many Perezes are in Spain."

"For me you'll always be matador," fluted John. "By the way when I made inquiries I found you used to be called Miguelito de Triana."

"That," said Miguelito, "was one of the stupid tricks of Manolo, my manager. It is romantic to be born in Triana in Seville, and stupid people think if you are born in Triana then you will be a torero, and Manolo he tried that with me. Then there was also the great Gitanillo de Triana." He looked round Jermyn Street: he was certainly away from the bulls. "But when I became famous everybody said Miguelito and Miguelito and nobody think more of Triana, which is good. I was born on a finca outside Puerto de Santa Maria."

"It is bliss to be with you," cried John and they reached the little, typically English pub which looked like a spick-and-span modern public lavatory in any part of the world.

"Will it be beer?" asked John who liked to invest as little as possible. "Good old English beer?"

"I drink much beer in Spain. Can I have whisky?"

"No, do have beer. Our English bitter is so different from your delicious Spanish beer. Two half pints of bitter, please."

"Yes, it is different beer," said Miguelito.

"Oh maestro," said John, pushing his wet lips almost against Miguelito's cheeks, "you could tell me and explain me so much. It isn't personal curiosity. It's for my book. Oh, you will have to see the manuscript. Of course when I have finished the book. I have such a good title for it. I'm going to call it Bulls, Bulls, And Bulls. Do you like it?"

"No," said Miguelito promptly.

"What a pity. Should I call it The Bull, The Torero And Death?"

"I don't like it but I know little of the books."

"Of books, not of the books, but I must say you speak good English. Now where did you pick it up?"

"One saint English lady teached me."

"Taught, matador, taught. But I wish I knew as much of bulls as you of English. There are so many questions I want to ask. I don't want to pester you but do answer one. Are you afraid when you go into the ring?"

"I am not afraid : I fight no more."

"Yes, yes, but when you fought?"

"I don't know," said Miguelito. "I am afraid of the public because I have responsibility to the public, I am afraid of the corrida before the corrida but when with the bull there is no time for me to be afraid. There is only the bull and I, and please, my sir, I am in England not to speak of the bull."

"How remiss of me," whined John. "I am turning your trip to England into a busman's holiday."

Miguelito hadn't the vaguest idea what a busman's holiday was, on the other hand he noticed that John was doing nothing to have their mugs refilled, so he ordered another round, and then paid for two more rounds. John seemed transparently short of cash. After a while John became aware that Miguelito was getting ready to leave, therefore something had to be done about it.

"Have you many friends in London?" he asked.

"Only two," said Miguelito thinking of Micky and Ted Cook, and wondered whether the preposterous Mrs. Cook had really locked him out.

"You'll have to meet some of mine, and first of all you'll meet my sister Thelma. I'm going to ring her up. She'll go mad about meeting a great matador. She's been for a fortnight to Majorca. She simply adores Spain and the Spaniards. Can I use the telephone?"

"This is my private telephone," said the pubkeeper. "There's a public one just round the corner."

"Would anybody be so ungracious in Spain?" asked John in a whisper and Miguelito shook his head.

John had to wait while a man with a brief-case carried on a long telephone conversation. He waited impatiently and in fear lest the matador would escape him. At last the man came out, pushed him smartly aside, and when John recovered his equilibrium he went in to ring up his sister.

"Listen, Thelma," he said, "I want you to come at once to the Six Coachmen. You know where it is?"

"I know every pub in London," she said wearily. "Why do you want me to come? Is," she asked excitedly, "Geoffrey back?"

"No, Geoffrey isn't back. You do bore all of us with Geoffrey. I want you to come because I've got just the man for you, a famous matador."

"A famous what?"

"Matador, bullfighter."

"That sounds thrilling. Is he wearing his fancy-dress?"

"Don't be an idiot, Thelma. Of course he isn't, and he must have heaps and heaps of money, and if you're nice to him I bet he'll take us out to lunch."

"As long as I don't have to pay for it as usual," said Thelma, promised to come, and rang off.

Her last remark annoyed her brother. It was no fault of his that sporadic writing didn't pay; it was neither his fault that they took so little of his work for television nor

that his travel book on Malta had been a flop;
certainly it wasn't of his doing that eight years ago
Thelma's husband fell off a steam roller on which
he had taken a joy-ride during a country holiday, and
was flattened to death, leaving her a life interest in his
estate, not much but enough to pay for her brother's
meals now and then.

After nearly an hour Thelma jerked her way into the
Six Coachmen. She moved as if she were taking small
unsuccessful leaps. She was slim though with big breasts
and did everything she could to hide them. Generally she
wore a shawl over her coat, which gave her an unkempt
appearance. She had fine eyes, an intelligent mouth and
good teeth. She thinks with her mouth, her enemies often
said. She came in on the defensive, for in spite of her
resolute nature she was shy on the surface. In her world
she dominated because she had a little more money than
others; outside her world it took her time to find her feet.
She found Miguelito handsome but outlandish, and she
didn't find it reassuring to be in the presence of a bullfighter for the simple reason that she hadn't been in the
presence of a matador before. She talked of Majorca and
of the one day she had spent in Barcelona. In order to
find her footing quicker she asked Miguelito and her
brother to have a drink with her. Miguelito blushed,
saying he had never in his life accepted a drink from a
woman.

"That shows you're not from here," she said.

Her conversation was of people whom Miguelito didn't
know. It was of men leaving women, women leaving
men, men not getting on with women and women not
getting on with men. Miguelito sat in silence staring at
the table, and John tried to bring the conversation round
to bulls and the corrida, or at least round to Spain, but

his efforts were of no avail. Miguelito was on the verge of going when Thelma, owing to the heat of the pub, by then very crowded, took her shawl off and he saw the shape of her bosom.

"You both, please," he said with his eyes on her protruding breasts, "will come and lunch with me, please? Yes, please."

"We should love to," said brother and sister in unison.

"You please choose place," said Miguelito and by accord they took him to an expensive restaurant in Jermyn Street.

The maître d'hôtel came, Miguelito asked them to order whatever they wanted to eat, for he for one would have consommé and a sole : he ate little. Thelma, now pleased with him because of the desire in his eyes, smiled and said it was a pity he didn't eat more; then she ordered for herself, foie gras, langouste and caneton à l'orange with a soufflé to follow. As she and John gave their orders Miguelito wrote figures down on a piece of paper. The foie gras and the consommé were first to come, Miguelito looked at his figures, and handed a sum of money to the waiter.

"I beg your pardon, sir?" said the waiter staring at the money.

"This is to pay for one consommé and two foies gras," said Miguelito, surprised by all the people staring at him.

"I don't understand you," said Thelma. "Why do you want to give that money?"

"I learn in England one pay when it is given," said Miguelito.

"Oh my God," cried John, "I see it all. Oh I can see it all. In a civilised country like Spain you pay in pubs when you leave, here of course they make you pay as they hand you your drink, and our great matador, the inimitable Miguelito, thought the same applies to food in restaurants, and he isn't so wrong. In all the awful cafeterias you pay before you're allowed to eat, but not here, matador. Keep your money till the end."

A woman laughed at the next table, which annoyed Thelma, so she said in a loud voice : "Tell me, toreador, a famous man like you of course knows everybody of importance in Spain?"

"And in Mexico," said her brother which stopped the woman laughing.

Thelma's eyes often met those of Miguelito during the meal. It would be, she thought, a novelty to go to bed with a bullfighter, and the bullfighter was a Spaniard too and she, as far back as she could remember, hadn't been to bed with a Spaniard either. It would be the case of the two birds. But why were his eyes glued to her ugly flabby bosom, of which she was so ashamed? She remembered having been told that Spaniards liked their women fat.

"Is it true," she asked, "that you Spanish men like women to be fat?"

"Many times we do," said Miguelito.

"In that case I don't think I'd have any success with Spaniards. Look at my arms, for instance, they're scraggy."

"I look at your arm," said Miguelito staring hard at her bosom. Antonio was right, and her eyes said she understood him. Miguelito looked anxiously at the brother, who, however, was engrossed in an evening paper. After a while he looked up.

"Always looking for copy," he sighed. "Matador, do you want to do me a favour?" Miguelito's nod implied he was ready to do the brother any favour. "Then, please, let me ring up the evening papers and tell them you are here in England on a visit and you have retired from the corrida."

"Oh, yes please," said Thelma. "I want to see your photograph in the papers."

"And I could make a little money," said John.

"Please no," said Miguelito. "If you do, I go." And he was ready to leave the table.

"Of course I won't if you don't want me to," said John. "You are so kind, I can't let you down. I can't, I can't and can't." Miguelito shook his hand. "Oh how kind of you. You are so much warmer than we are."

His sister was of the same opinion. When she couldn't eat any more, she remembered she had an appointment with her hairdresser. "If you feel lonely tonight," she said, "ring up towards seven. I am doing nothing tonight." She gave him her telephone number and with ungainly steps hurried from the restaurant.

"What a pity my sister is so untidy in body and mind," remarked John.

Miguelito said nothing. Later John suggested that if Miguelito had nothing better to do, he should accompany him to a picture gallery. He made the offer apologetically and was astonished by the matador's prompt acceptance, was even more astonished when in the gallery he saw the interest Miguelito took in the pictures, and an intelligent interest at that.

"I didn't know," he said, "that matadors were interested in any art except their own." He hoped that was tactful enough.

"The outside world," said Miguelito smiling, "especially foreigners, take us for rare insects. There are of course toreros who remain simple and don't want to educate themselves, but I say in all modesty a man must be very intelligent to be a good torero. You must have intelligence to know what like is the bull, what to do with him, and how to act—is it react?—quickly. So we can understand other things too. There is a famous matador who to spend his time when not doing fights studied law. Now he is a full lawyer, but only for his pleasure."

A few weeks with Miguelito, thought John, would reveal for him secrets no one else in England knew. At six o'clock Miguelito remembered he was meeting his two friends, and asked John whether he wanted to come too.

"I should love to," said John. "Are they Spanish?"

"No, English," and John's face fell when Miguelito introduced him to Micky and Ted Cook. The meeting was a failure. Micky with his Irish sense of freedom managed not to feel uneasy, but both John and Ted Cook did. John tried to talk down to Ted hoping that would smooth matters, and as a result Ted soon decided it was time for him to go to the missus.

"A very great pity to me you are going," said Miguelito, "but you will come tomorrow, please?"

"I'll try to, sir," said Ted and was glad to go.

"So you are the manager of the hotel?" John asked Micky.

"Manager my arse," said Micky trying to imitate John's movement with his hands. "I'm the maid-of-all-work, and there is only a manageress, an old bitch who leaves all the work to me."

"Oh good," said John because he didn't know what else to say.

"Mr. Spaniard, my friend," said Micky to Miguelito, "I must go back now. There must be about ten of them waiting on the doorstep. I'll be seeing you in the morning. Here's a latchkey—be good."

He left without saying goodbye to John, who now took Miguelito's arm, leaned over him like a weeping willow over a river and spoke in serious tones.

"Miguelito, you are still a stranger here," he said, "so you will allow me to give you advice, and to make suggestions how to steer your course."

"Yes?" said Miguelito, fearing he would forbid him to meet his sister tonight.

"Here in England," went on John, "life is different to life in Spain. It is less free, there are far more barriers. These two men you were chatting with and whom you called your friends aren't the people for you to know and to go about with."

"Why? What they do?"

"Nothing, but they are of a different world to yours, therefore there is a great dividing line between you. You shouldn't cross it."

"Mister John," said Miguelito with his charming smile of determination, "I will say one thing for you. My friends are my friends and if I want rather to go with one shoe-black than with a duke I go. I go with him in my country in Spain, so I go with you in your country, a country not my country. I look for the heart in the man, not for title or moneys. These two my friends."

"Oh well," said John abashed. "Of course if you feel like it . . ."

"I feel."

"Sorry," said John blushing deeply, and Miguelito who saw the blush patted his shoulder.

"Women perhaps think like that in Spain," said Miguelito, "man doesn't."

"Perhaps I'm a woman," said John, and laughed shrilly, another point Miguelito missed.

"Perhaps I know much of man," said Miguelito looking at the clock. "You, friend, you know not the many mans . . ."

"Men," said John and laughed again.

"Men, thank you. A torero with some success has many hundred men on him all the time. Some real aficionados of his art, many others just to take money. Miguelito, my mother ill, give, please, hundred duros. Miguelito, my commerce go bad, give two hundred duros, Miguelito, you wonderful, give five hundred duros."

"And what do you do?" asked John with almost professional interest.

"I give. Why say no if I can give?"

"You are wonderful and I don't want five hundred duros. Not at present at least," he added honestly.

"Why not give?" said Miguelito. "One day come a bull, he kill you and you lie dying and then say now what I will do with money I didn't give?"

John was deeply moved. His nature yearned for great men and saints, whom he seldom encountered. In Miguelito he felt he had found both. He hadn't enough money to buy another round as a sign of his gratitude for having met Miguelito, so, rather shyly, he suggested he would come to the hotel every morning, if the matador felt so disposed, and improve his English.

"You must become perfect in English as you're perfect in everything else," he said and gratefully Miguelito patted his shoulder. "Look, it's seven. Ring up my sister, if you want to."

With a sigh of relief Miguelito rushed to the telephone. He had observed the time too but was shy before the brother. Thelma answered the telephone and told him to meet her in a pub near the Brompton Oratory.

"Where, please?"

"Of course you wouldn't know where the Oratory is. How funny somebody not knowing where the Oratory is. Aren't you a Catholic? I thought all Spaniards are Catholic."

"I am Catholic but why please?"

"The Oratory is in Knightsbridge. Do you know where Knightsbridge is at least?"

"No, thank you."

"For God's sake send John to the telephone. He'll put you into a taxi or something."

It was John who put him into a cab and before closing the door he said to him: "Take it easy, matador. My sister is a will-o'-the-wisp but made of cotton wool."

He closed the door pleased with himself: a will-o'-the-wisp made of cotton wool. He would use that in his writing. As he was a good young man in his way he hoped the cotton wool wouldn't choke Miguelito if he took a bite, and he began to regret he had introduced him to Thelma.

Miguelito found the pub dreary and she kept him waiting for a good half hour. He watched men in overcoats drinking beer and reading the evening papers; he saw women, tired from offices, drinking a little gin and tonic, also reading the evening papers with scarcely any of the morning's make-up left on their faces; and Thelma came in not wearing her shawl.

"I'm sorry to be late," she said. "Now where shall we dine?"

"Dine?" he asked. "I eat one time only the day."

"Do you mean to say you ask out a girl in the evening without inviting her to dinner? Have you no money? If you haven't I'll pay for it. It won't be the first time either."

"No money?" said Miguelito. "I have money, plenty."

He laughed. "Plenty more than I want, but I not eat in evenings, one meal every day."

"Well, then you can watch me eat," said Thelma. "Come on. And," she added, hating the merriment in his eyes, "you don't have to pay for it either."

"Because have no money," he said and roared with laughter. As good a cachondeo as he had ever heard. Manolo would collapse with mirth if he heard that an English lady thought he would let her pay for her dinner. On second thoughts he had to admit that English ladies seemed very interested in money. Thelma didn't care for his high spirits; for within herself she knew she wasn't much of a person and the fear of the ridiculous and the fear of not understanding pursued her doggedly. Money, especially, was a ticklish point with her. It gave her power but she knew it gave her the power she longed for only with those who had less than she. It was all complicated and often in a turmoil, and the only way out she knew was to go to bed with the men in whose company she felt insecure.

"How much money do they pay you for those bull-fights?" she asked in the taxi.

"Nothing, I no more fight."

"But when you did fight?"

"Often eight hundred thousand pesetas. In Mexico much more."

"Wait," she said and changed in her mind the pesetas into pounds. "What," she exclaimed, nearly hitting the roof as she jumped, "nearly eight thousand pounds? I can't believe it. Christ, it's my income for eight years. And how long have you to fight for that?"

"Twice twenty minutes."

She moaned, her hand was unable to resist caressing the arm of so highly paid a man. The highly paid man immediately touched her breast. With little conviction she pushed the hand away.

"But now you don't fight any more, so there is no more money," she said.

"No more money," he said wishing she would let him stroke her breast instead of talking of money. "No money come, if I not fight. You beautiful, you guapa," and the hand shot out.

"Not here in the taxi," said Thelma. "I hate being pawed in taxis. But did you put any money aside?"

"I have forty-five million pesetas," said Miguelito thinking that even the *putas* in the Calle Postigo in the Puerto spoke less of money; but who was he to judge an English lady with such desirable breasts?

That was too much for Thelma. She was no gold-digger, in fact in her life money flowed in one direction, namely away from her. It was the essence of that large sum, for her quite impersonal, which filled her with awe and respect though not for Miguelito : just for the money.

"I suppose," she said hopefully, "you can't get it out of Spain?"

"No, but I have money in America, dollars, bank from America send dollars here."

He had an answer to everything, and with sad fatalism she didn't mind him stroking her breast. With this man she couldn't compete, consequently she could do but one thing with him, that is to lie down when the time came. She took him to a Greek restaurant in Chelsea believing there must be some affinity between Greeks and Spaniards. Miguelito repeated he couldn't eat; she, however, ate heartily. He drank wine and his eyes were on her, heavy with desire. Now and then her remarks dumb-founded him, and if he hadn't known that she was John's sister, and if Antonio hadn't warned him, he would have taken her for a woman of ill repute. She could be gay and amusing, and now she excelled herself, which was the first of her offerings to forty-five million pesetas and God knew how many dollars, of which, in fact, she wanted none; and Miguelito fell completely under her spell. His right hand clasped hers. It was a cool hand, and she liked its touch. With the wine she began to notice that he was handsome, but looks mattered little to her. In her relations with men she alone mattered for herself. The man could be clumsy in love or ugly to look at : as long as she was satisfied with her own performance she was content.

"Why don't you fight any more?" she asked. "Can't you or aren't you allowed?"

"I can if I want but I don't want."

"You mean if you wanted to you could right now earn eight hundred thousand pesetas?"

"This moment not, bull season over, but even with bull season I much more like sit with you." He kissed her hand.

"Cut that cackle out. Really I can't understand anybody sitting here if he could make about eight thousand pounds by being somewhere else."

"I love you," said Miguelito.

"I like you too," she said.

She lived not far from Thurloe Square, and when the cab took them to her door, Miguelito got out with her. He held her arm while he paid the driver. "I suppose," sighed Thelma, "you will come up and then we both know what will happen."

Her flat appeared strange to him. It was untidy and the drawing-room, full of sofas and more chairs than were strictly necessary for at least three dozen people, gave the impression of a second-class waiting-room in a station.

There were a number of looking glasses on the walls, some cracked, some with broken frames and two of value. Dead chrysanthemums bowed their heads in an imitation Japanese vase. The carpet had a hole, and in the passage there was an assortment of luggage, as though she had just moved in and hadn't yet time to unpack.

"It's all in a mess," she said, "but I don't like being in. I sleep here and when I get up in the morning I go out at once."

"Where?"

"To pubs, to see friends. I live through my friends. But sometimes I give parties here. You must come to my next party."

He took her in his arms and kissed her with force. She laughed. "The real he-man stuff," she said. "The full-blooded Spaniard." He kissed her again. "Not yet," she said pulling away. "I'll get you a drink first."

For the soulful hour had come, the hour to discuss life and death. Geoffrey never went to bed with her without indulging in such-like talk, which she considered erudite, sophisticated and highbrow. She wanted to know what Miguelito thought of life and death. She brought in a bottle of cheap Italian wine, sat down on sofa number five, and told Miguelito to sit down beside her. He did so, putting his arm round her waist.

"What is it you want most in life?" she asked.

"You."

"Please be serious. You'll have me, don't worry, but I want to know what you want most in life."

"To be away from them," said Miguelito.

"From them? Who are they?"

"They are many, very many."

"I don't know who they are, but just to be away is negative. What is it you want positively? What are your aspirations? Which is your road?"

"I don't understand," said Miguelito.

"What a pity," she said, "but you must learn. I'll teach you. We are all on a road, we often come to cross-roads, and have to choose. We can't choose if we don't know our goal, if we don't know where we want to go, and there is often a force stronger than ourselves which pushes us along, and unbeknown to us we might be treading the right road." She saw that he was not listening but sat with vacant eyes, and a frown between his eyes gave him a sulky look. His hand played half-heartedly with her breast. "Oh well," she said, "you don't seem to be interested. I suppose you are happy with your millions, so we'd better drink this up and go to bed. What a pity."

He had spoiled her hour but in bed she rather liked him. Towards dawn she woke up. He was lying beside her covered with sweat, groaning.

"Are you having a nightmare, darling?" she asked, poking him.

He jumped up, still asleep, and bounded in the direction of the window. He knocked against a chair and woke up. He stood shivering, she had already switched on the light, and he smiled at her apologetically, not quite sure who she was. It didn't occur to her, as she watched him curiously, that perhaps he knew the goal and which road to tread.

CHAPTER SIX

"D OCE CASCABELES tiene mi caballo," sang Lolita, and the telephone bell rang. She didn't bother to answer it before she reached "por la carretera," then she swung her hips and bottom across the room, her legs on the marble floor swinging to the rhythm of the song.

"Who is it?" she asked. "Oh, it's you, Manolo." She laughed. "What is it you want?"

"Have you heard from him?"

"I have," she said. "He sent me a picture postcard of an open bridge with ships under it. Why do they open bridges there? They must be mad."

"What is his address?"

"He gives no address. Probably he's already on his way back. I knew it wouldn't last."

"Stupid woman, of course it will last." He consulted somebody, she could hear the whispers but couldn't make out the words. "Lolita," said Manolo now, "we are coming round."

"Who are we?"

"You'll see."

"I'm not curious but come, old hog."

She went and sat down again. She thought of smoking a cigarette but to get up was too much of an effort. On a table within reach lay a used toothpick, which she took and chewed, and that kept her busy till the bell rang. Her sister was out shopping in the warm November afternoon but an old woman who, though she had no official status in the house, liked to spend her days there went to open the door when the bell tinkled in the patio. She looks like a statue of laziness, thought Manolo as they came in. There were seven of them.

"Now this is rich," roared Lolita, "only the mono-sabios are missing."

"There is no more need for the monosabios," said Manolo darkly. "No more dead bulls will be dragged from the plaza."

"Take wine to the dining room," shouted Lolita to the old woman, "and come with me caballeros, into my dining room, and there sit down."

The dining room had heavy furniture painted in black, and brass and wrought iron were much in evidence. Lolita loved the dining room. The men sat down round the table and she eyed them without interest. There they were, the whole lot of them : the three peons, the two picadors, Joaquin, the fatter of them, worse for wine than the others, and the eager and depressed Paco, the mozo de espada. They sat and nobody spoke till Lolita asked them how they got together.

"I asked them to meet me," said Manolo. "I wanted to exchange opinions with them. Then we thought we might come and see you and exchange opinions with you."

"What about?" asked Lolita, emptying her glass with a clucking noise.

"Miguelito, woman," said Manolo. "Can't you understand we miss him?"

"It's more than I do," she said laughing. "He'll come back when he wants to and if he doesn't come back I won't die because of him. It is quieter here without him."

"If you weren't a great lady," hissed Manolo, "I might call you by a very coarse word." But that made Lolita only laugh more. "We must get in touch with him."

"He has sent me this postcard," said Joaquin, showing her the picture of a Life Guardsman on horseback with the inscription : "Would you like a horse like that, Joaquin?" "I will treasure it." He banged the table. "I've worked for other toreros, some very famous, but never for one like him. He is exceptional."

"You speak?" said Luis. "I was with him for ten years and there never was such a master of the lidia. Lolita, for ten seasons I stood in the burladero, my eyes on him, following every movement of his, and whenever I had to take the bull off—you remember, Manolo, in the Monumental when the bull lifted him and everybody thought it was the end? And when he was badly gored in Cordoba?—yes, whenever I had to take the bull off, I felt as if I were doing it for my mother."

"He must come back to us," shrieked Paco, still too young to be accustomed to wine. "He is all I have."

"Be quiet, boy," said Manolo. "This will take us nowhere."

"I don't understand it," said Luis the peon who had a dark Moorish face and agonised eyes. "I can understand that a man wants to retire, but to give up this friendship, the love we gave him and he gave us . . . no, I can't understand it."

"Perhaps something happened in him," said Juan, the third peon. "We know so little, it's all in the hands of God. I pray for him a lot."

"Why don't you all start crying?" asked Lolita with her elbows on the table.

"We thought he might have given you his address," said Manolo.

"He hasn't," she said. "Don't bother too much. He'll get sick of those bridges which open, and he'll want to come back to his Lolita. Anyway, I am told all English women are ugly. They look like brooms. A sailor told me that : he's been there."

"That's still to be seen," said Manolo.

"What do you mean?" asked Lolita and mockery left her eyes. "Do you know anything?" she shrieked.

"Nothing, don't get upset."

"Then shut up, you old hog."

Manolo made a mental note that Lolita's possessiveness might some day be of use; her jealousy too, but first it would have to be truly awakened. "We must know where he is. That is the beginning."

"What is it you really want?" asked Lolita. "Can't you give him a little rest?"

"Eternal rest," said Joaquin, swallowing hard.

"He is the centre of our lives," said Luis. "I don't think of money, I only want to be with him and serve him."

"He must come back," screamed Paco and was told to shut up.

Lolita looked at the glum men and yawned. She wanted, besides, to go to the cinema. "What about a little singing and dancing?" she asked. "He isn't dead yet."

"Señorita," began Paco but Joaquin put his hand on his mouth.

"There is one person who might know," said Manolo, "and that's Don Antonio. I'll go and see if he is in the Casino, but I don't want you all to come with me."

"We wasted our time," said the peon when the old woman let them out.

"I didn't waste mine," said Manolo.

"I don't follow you," said Joaquin, who was huge in his drunkenness with the setting sun behind him.

"Of course you don't," said Manolo. "Do you suppose if you had my brain you'd be a picador?"

Joaquin wanted to answer but words failed to come his way, so he muttered something about managers being all crooks, and then taking the arm of Bartolo, the other picador, he staggered away. In about ten minutes' time he found the words he was feverishly searching for.

"Manolo," he said, "is the bald-headed son of a whore."

Bartolo agreed and they both felt better.

The peons and Paco accompanied Manolo as far as the Casino, where they left him, after they had all promised each other to keep in touch, and the one who got the address first would communicate with the others. Manolo was resolved not to keep his promise if it suited him strategically. But the sadness of Paco moved him.

"Chico," he said, "have you spent all your money? Is that why you are so sad? If you need some just ask me for it."

"I don't need money, I need him." He pointed at the tower of the Giralda, on which dusk was surreptitiously descending. "How can he cast himself away from it?" asked the little Sevillano in a choking voice.

"Haven't you heard there are bridges there which open? Perhaps he prefers them. Cheer up, boy, I'll get him back somehow. Go with God, and you'll soon hear from me."

Antonio was sitting in the Casino with friends, men of importance, and Manolo approached them with becoming modesty. Antonio asked him to sit down with them but Manolo said he didn't wish to disturb the caballeros : he only wanted a word or two with Don Antonio.

"I know what you want," said Antonio as they moved away. "It is his address, what?"

"How clever you are, Don Antonio."

"Clever or not clever, I won't give it to you. He wrote to ask me not to, and till I think it is my duty by him to give you his address, you won't have it and it's no good asking for it. He even asked me not to write to him, and gave me his address in case he might be urgently needed." Antonio's eyes sparkled : a cachondeo was coming. "Now if you threw yourself in front of a tram and the tram cut your legs off, then of course I would cable him. So why don't you do that?"

"And if he doesn't come then what will I do with my cut-off legs?" asked Manolo, who considered himself anybody's equal where a cachondeo was concerned. They laughed and shoulders were slapped. "But," said Manolo, becoming serious again, "don't you think it's unnatural?"

"It is, but what can we do about it? Don't forget you and I have never been toreros. I once fought a heifer at a tienta, and retired for life. Come and have a drink with us."

I must think up some emergency, Manolo decided, and keep near to Antonio.

"Have you any news of Miguelito?" one of the men of importance asked him.

"He is on a trip to northern Europe," said Manolo, "studying the native customs. He is a very studious man."

CHAPTER SEVEN

O N THE seventh day of their affair Thelma suggested to Miguelito he should move into her flat. Miguelito refused. He hadn't lived in a woman's house except his own mother's, and he wouldn't do so now. She took it calmly, and said if he liked the discomfort of going away every morning it was, after all, his business. Miguelito nearly told her that he didn't live even with Lolita when he was in Seville : he would spend his nights and part of the day with her, but he still stayed in the Andalusia Palace.

"I wish he weren't so possessive and he takes everything so seriously," confided Thelma to a friend. "What will he do when Geoffrey comes back?"

"He'll take a knife and kill him," said the friend, a blonde with spectacles who wouldn't have minded getting to know the Spaniard better.

"That's all story-book nonsense," said Thelma. "I've been to Majorca, so I know my Spaniards, but he is a nuisance at times. The other evening he stormed at me because I brought Roger along. Then last night he made a scene because Frankie sat down at our table at Prunier's. Frankie, darling. Surely he could see at once that Frankie is a queer."

It wasn't easy for Miguelito either. In a remarkably short time he had forgotten Antonio's injunction, and had persuaded himself into believing that Thelma gave herself to him because she loved him beyond measure. He

began seriously to ask himself whether it wasn't his duty
to marry his friend's sister, who gave her most treasured
possession to him. He listened little to John's lessons; his
chats with Micky were cut short to run to the telephone
and speak to Thelma, who when she telephoned him
spoke in a painful voice. Yet his English was rapidly
improving. Ted Cook faded out of his life because he
found no time to visit pubs on his own. He visited plenty
in Thelma's company. Her friends didn't warm to him,
took, in fact, little notice of him. Theirs was a closed
small world with shuttered windows. New faces, especially a face from Spain, mattered nothing to them, and
when they heard he was a matador they thought that
was as good a joke as any. She took him to an after-
dinner party where everybody got drunk, nobody spoke
to him, and two fights developed after midnight.

"You look bored and you know nobody here," said
Thelma, who was enjoying herself. "Take the key of the
flat and wait for me."

"No," he said, "I wait for nobody. You come now."

"My Spaniard," she said in a loud voice, "is so jealous
that if I don't go at once he will knife me." The party
laughed. "It's like living with a sheik of Araby."

"Don't you," he asked her in the cab, "want a life of
peace, a life for a woman, children?"

"I do," she said. "Everybody knows I do, but what
can I do when all these people are badgering me?"

She kissed his hand, which was a trick of hers, and he
was mollified. He couldn't understand that a woman of
thirty odd years had no children, and as the days went
by he became obsessed with the idea that God had sent
him to England to redeem her from her vacant existence
which he couldn't believe she enjoyed. On the tenth day

he decided to consult her brother. If her brother believed it was his duty to marry her, then he would do so.

"John," he said before the English lesson began, "I want to talk to you. It's about your sister."

"Miguelito," said John, "don't talk to me of my sister. I gather you see a good deal of her and I'd ease up on her if I were you. I told you she was a will-o'-the-wisp but made of cotton wool. She should be hung on a Christmas-tree in a suburban home. Had I known we should become such great friends"—he had already borrowed twenty pounds off Miguelito—"I wouldn't have introduced you to her. You don't know how hard it is in the beginning. Once I told a man whom I didn't expect to meet again a stupid lie, then saw him by accident every day, and of course the lie was found out. The same is happening now. Don't speak of her to me, dear, dear Miguelito. She isn't a bad sort, but do take her lightly. There is no substance."

"Should I marry her?" asked Miguelito.

"Marry her?" shrieked John. "Never. Do you understand me? Never."

"You are not much brother," said Miguelito.

"Not much of a brother," said John. "No and no and no. Now let us go on with shall and will."

"I shall if she needs me."

"She doesn't."

What does he know, said Miguelito to himself. A woman who gives her body as she does, certainly loves you, and she is a poor lonely thing, and marriage and motherhood would redeem her. He didn't learn in the course of the lesson the difference between will and shall. Anyway the two at the moment meant the same to him.

Thelma was going to lunch with a woman friend, so

they would meet only in the evening. As a matter of fact she didn't lunch with the woman friend because when she was ready to go out to meet her, Geoffrey, the love of her soul and mind and now and then of her body, rang up.

"I am back," he said. "I want to see you at once. What's this about a Spaniard and a bullfighter to boot?"

"I'll tell you everything, darling."

"Then come at once to the Moonbeam."

"I'm coming," she panted, and the woman friend waited for an hour and then left, cursing stupid, harum-scarum Thelma.

Thelma dined with Miguelito, and when they arrived at the flat and sat down in the second-class waiting-room, she casually remarked that an old friend would be looking in for a drink.

"Please don't," said Miguelito. "Telephone him not to come. I want to be alone with you."

"We can't be alone all the time. I've given you enough of my time. I'm not a hermit crab."

"Crab? But I must speak to you tonight of important matters."

"Here he is," she said, and ran from the room to answer the bell. He shook his head, for it was difficult to understand her. Lolita gave herself because she was made for giving herself, but this English lady, who gave herself with such passion. . . . Thelma came in with Geoffrey.

Geoffrey was tall, wore glasses, had black hair, a fine profile, reviewed books in weeklies, and had been a Party member. He had a high opinion of himself, and loved himself for being bitingly intolerant. He took an immediate dislike to the Spaniard, whom he judged to be easy game. After the two men were introduced to each other he sat down on sofa number three beside Thelma and put his arm round her shoulder, crossed his legs, pulled his right trouser leg up to the knee and said to her with his eyes on Miguelito: "Scratch my leg. I've got the itch again." Dutifully she began to scratch his rather white leg, smiling at Miguelito at the same time. Miguelito was still standing.

"Thank you, sweetie pie," said Geoffrey. "She scratches divinely," he said to Miguelito, smiling. Miguelito didn't answer. "I gather from Thelma," said Geoffrey, "that you are a Spaniard. And she said something to the effect that you are a toreador? Can that be true?"

"It can't be," said Miguelito. "There is no person called in Spanish toreador. One is first a novillero, and when one takes the alternativa then one is a matador, both toreros, but never toreador. That comes from a French novel."

"You read books too?" said Geoffrey, smiling at his prey. "I thought people who kill bulls didn't read books."

"You are mistaken, many do," said Miguelito, and Thelma watched them, her mouth half open, her right hand playing with her pearls.

"Well, well," said Geoffrey, "all this is very interesting and I suppose I should change my mind about you gentlemen. I don't think I will. It needs ignorance, cruelty and crass stupidity to kill innocent animals."

"But he gets eight thousand pounds for killing a bull," said Thelma nestling closer to Geoffrey.

"For two bulls," said Miguelito who, in order to calm himself, had decided Geoffrey was a relation.

"Two bulls," said Geoffrey. "Not one but two. Well, well, and I get ten guineas for reviewing four mucky novels. But I've read somewhere you chaps believe you are artists."

"He always says that," said Thelma, "though I can't see how."

"Please," said Miguelito, "I don't want to talk of bulls. I came to England so as not to talk of bulls."

"I don't care a damn why you came to England," said Geoffrey, "and I didn't ask you to come to England either." Like other Party members he became a patriot when it suited him. "You should have stayed in your brutal, bloodthirsty, reactionary country and gone on killing innocent animals."

"Geoffrey, darling, you are going too far," said Thelma who was enjoying herself. "Don't let him pull your leg, Miguelito."

"I'm pulling nobody's leg," said Geoffrey. "What I want to tell this man here is that to be a bullfighter is an offence against the civilised world. Do you understand me? Or are you too woolly to understand me?"

"I don't mind what you think of me," said Miguelito, "but don't speak bad of my country, please."

"Your country?" said Geoffrey, who was becoming aware he was going too far. "Your country stinks."

Quietly Miguelito lifted him out of the sofa, and as his arm was round Thelma's waist he thus lifted her a little too. Once Geoffrey was on his feet Miguelito knocked him down, and Geoffrey crumpled up, then stretched himself in full length above the hole in the carpet, and a trickle of blood left his open mouth. He began to sob.

"Geoffrey is right," shrieked Thelma. "You are a brute, you are uncivilised. Get out and I never want to set eyes on you again, you violent murderer."

"But my love," said Miguelito, "he insults my country. I mind not what he say to me, but not Spain. But now

I hit him it is over. I'll help him up and forget."

"No," she shouted, "you get out. It's over. Only a fool like you couldn't see he is the only man I love. I was just killing time with you. Go."

"Yes, I go," said Miguelito. He looked back from the door : she was kneeling beside Geoffrey. On the stairs his mind was void of thoughts. He saw a pub conveniently facing the house, and it was after his second whisky that it came home to him he had been a fool from the word go, which word had been uttered by him. Marriage and children. Mi pobre Miguelito, he said to himself, you've made a fool of yourself, you didn't listen to Antonio, you thought you knew better. These English women aren't for you, with a Lolita you know where you are, with a Thelma you don't because you understand nothing, you sentimental idiot. Still now you know where she is. She is in that horrible man's arms, her breasts against him; and he crashed his glass to the floor.

"I say," said the pubkeeper leaning over the counter.

"Sorry it is fallen," said Miguelito quickly. Perhaps the man was right—he wasn't civilised. He began to pick up the debris.

"That's all right, sir," said the pubkeeper. "Just two bob. Shall I serve you another whisky?"

"Yes, please," said Miguelito.

If going to bed indiscriminately with men was a sign of civilisation, then he preferred uncivilised Lolita who did it because it was her profession. He now longed for her, for his friends, for Seville, for the shadow of the Giralda, for Antonio, even for . . . No, that was out of the question. He shouldn't think of it. Yet he must think of it because she was, probably at the very moment, clapping horns on his forehead. To run from the bulls in order to become a bull oneself. I am a bull, he wanted to say to the man standing next to him at the bar, but he remembered Antonio's words: "In England," he had said, "it is no offence to call a man a bull. They call themselves John Bull, and it would be difficult to explain to them that we who call the bull a noble animal which he is, call a cuckold a bull." So he didn't say to the man next to him he was a bull.

Marriage and motherhood, and now she was in that odious man's arms. He suddenly wanted to go back and make a fearful scene, so he took a cab and drove back to the hotel, slunk up the stairs in fear of meeting Micky and having to explain why he had come back so early, then in bed he called Thelma a puta fifty times but that brought no sleep. If only his friends were with him. Before dawn came he decided to keep away from all English ladies for good. He would, while in England, frequent only prostitutes.

CHAPTER EIGHT

"WOULD YOU," he asked Micky in the morning, "say I am not civilised in the English way?"

"I don't know what the English way is: I'm Irish, but all I can say I have met some gents in my time and can tell you that you're the only real gentleman I ever met. So she gave you the boot?" Miguelito's eyes were vacant.

"So she sent you packing? Vamoose and all that?" Miguelito nodded. "Cheer up, as good fish in the sea and so on. But keep away from those dames. Listen, tonight I'm free, so we'll go to a dance hall right here in Tottenham Court Road and pick up a couple of Irish girls, but don't talk to them of anything, just hug them and then we'll bring them back here. Okidoke?"

"No more women, please," said Miguelito.

"Just leave it to me. You won't come to any harm if you take care of your wallet." The knocking on the wall became louder. "I'd better take his breakfast."

Miguelito lay in bed smoking one cigarette after the other. Thelma's torso floated above the cigarette smoke. In a little while Micky poked his head in to say John was waiting downstairs.

"I don't want to see him," said Miguelito.

Micky closed the door, then the door opened and John, looking every inch a penitent, slid into the room.

"Miguelito, my great matador," he said, "don't visit her sins on me. I would be lost without you."

"I don't want to speak to you, and I will tell you," he shouted, knowing that the final insult, after which there could be no reconciliation, was coming. "Your sister is a bad, disgraceful woman, a woman of no honour."

"I know, I know, Miguelito, but it's no fault of mine. I warned you. She is a poor thing, don't think of her but remain my idol."

Miguelito felt like throwing his hands up and in. If this was a country where one could speak like that to a brother of his sister, without the brother taking offence, then perhaps the country would remain an enigma for good, and he decided to take everything as it came along and to ask no more questions.

"What does idol mean?" he asked. "Sit down."

John grasped his hand and kissed it.

"In this country," said John, "there is one thing we are interested in, that is to have a good time. A good time comes first. If you want to stay among us, then imitate us and have a good time too."

"But," asked Miguelito, "honour, ideals, religion?"

"Those we only have in an emergency," laughed John. "When a ship goes down we are all heroes and say 'after you, please', and we are religious and sing hymns instead of building rafts. And if the ship of state founders," he said in a lugubrious voice, "then we give three cheers for St. George who wasn't English, and die on the playing fields of Winchester. You see I'm an Old Wykehamist." He was enjoying himself and if only an editor of some weekly asked him to write a humorous article on England he would use every word he had just said. "But, Miguelito," he added, "don't you say that to the English. They wouldn't like it."

"I understand: I am not English. That is why I hit

that man. We Spanish we can say what we like of Spain, and we many times say it, but not a foreigner."

"Which shows we're all very much the same," said John and nodded like the sage he felt himself to be at the moment.

"But I liked her very much," said Miguelito with a sigh.

"Forget her, and don't let even her memory interfere with our friendship," said John, and Miguelito asked John to lunch with him.

Micky was true to his word, and took Miguelito to an Irish dance hall where the police had twice to restore order in the course of the night. Micky picked up two hefty Irish girls, with whom the two of them caroused in Miguelito's room. One was called Kitty and she stayed in Miguelito's bed till the morning. She asked before she left whether they would meet in the evening.

"I don't know," he said airily. He was beginning to learn.

Before he went out there was a knock on the door, and because it was a knock he didn't know, his heart raced as he thought that it might be Thelma coming to repent, to explain that it had been a mistake, a misunderstanding, and she loved him with a heart which was racing just as much. The schoolmaster stood on the threshold.

"All my apologies, sir, for intruding," he said, "but you are a neighbour, and so I came to seek your advice."

"Please come in," said Miguelito.

"Thank you, thank you. Now, sir, have you noticed a strange, I should even say indecent apparition in this hotel? And that apparition must be living on this landing."

"Apparition?"

"Yes sir. A horrible sissy glides along the landing and down the stairs to the bathroom clad in silk, a most immoral sight. But in which room does he live? If we knew the room I should ask you to accompany me and we could order him to leave at once. A most shocking and disgraceful apparition."

"I don't know where he lives," said Miguelito.

"In that case I won't take up your time any longer, sir, but if you find out do let me know. It is in our interest that the queer should go."

"It is," said Miguelito, wondering whether the school-master on his way out would spot his red silk dressing gown which, when the schoolmaster had begun to speak, he had pushed off the chair. The schoolmaster didn't spot it. That made Miguelito's day, until in Great Russell Street he ran into Thelma, who was going to meet Geoffrey in a public house near the British Museum. Miguelito pretended to be looking at books in a pub-lisher's window. She stopped, not because she wanted to speak to him but because her nerves gave way.

"Oh, it's you," she said. "We needn't be enemies, you know. I hate being on bad terms with anybody. If an affair ends it ends, but one needn't be enemies."

Miguelito lifted his hat, then moved on, which he soon afterwards regretted; for it wasn't taking matters lightly.

The manageress of the hotel didn't take matters lightly either. On Saturday night there was such carousing in Miguelito's bedroom with two other hefty Irish girls who were both called Kitty, that it woke her up, and to the energetic tapping of the schoolmaster's fist on the wall, she burst into the room, the door of which they had for-gotten to lock. Micky and the girls were sitting on the bed, Miguelito was dancing a Sevillana for them, doing his own clapping. The manageress sacked Micky and told Miguelito to leave in the morning.

"I will take you as my servant of confidence," said Miguelito to Micky.

"I'll find you a good flat where you can dance to your heart's content," said Micky, "and in the evenings we'll get drunk and talk Oirish with these girls."

Miguelito lost all desire to dance, and the girls ceased to mean anything to him. He was drinking, drinking too much. He had always kept himself at a distance from the bottle, for he knew it could but interfere with his art, and he had lived for his art. Now he had none. He gripped the bottle of whisky and holding it up let the amber stream pour into his mouth.

"Steady, man," said Micky.

"That's how an outcast of the lidia should drink," said Miguelito and Micky put him to bed. Miguelito cried in his sleep.

"Well, my master," said Micky in the morning, "we're off now. I have done some telephoning and found in Jermyn Street the furnished flat you want. But it is expensive. Sixteen guineas a week, is that too much?"

"Nothing is too much," said Miguelito wondering whether his head would have mercy on him and disintegrate.

"You are rich then?" asked Micky.

"Yes, rich, and speak less."

"Will you take me with you when you go back to Spain?"

"I will never go to Spain."

"But why not? Are you in trouble?"

"In great trouble and speak less. I must sleep one hour more."

In an hour's time Micky roused him again. His head

had ceased to be his enemy, Micky packed, and they moved into a service flat with imitation Sheraton furniture in Jermyn Street. Micky said he would cook him stews when he didn't feel like going out. On the same landing was another flat with a woman living in it who had a beauty parlour in Knightsbridge. She was forty and elegant. After they had several times gone up together in the lift and she had found out he was a Spaniard, she asked him in for a drink.

"I go every year to Malaga for my holidays," she said, "and I love Spaniards, especially you Andalusians."

"We are very gay," said Miguelito.

On the following evening she returned his visit and stayed the night with him. "I could really fall in love with you," she said a few nights later, which made Miguelito shake with silent laughter.

"I could too," he said politely and rejoiced at having learned to enjoy the emptiness of life and love.

CHAPTER NINE

MIGUELITO TOOK to spending his afternoons in the National Gallery. He looked at the paintings with a sort of obsession, trying with unformulated words to question the long-dead painters. What did they feel when they painted? Did their paintings mean everything to them? Were they lonely when not painting? And when they couldn't paint any more or hadn't the courage to paint any more did they feel as he did? He tried to reassure himself by saying he had in his own medium acquired a sort of immortality too. They would speak of him now and then, writers on tauromachy would mention his name at times, and there were many alive to whom he had given glorious afternoons; and then he would wander on to another canvas. It was Friday afternoon and he left at lighting-up time with the rain trickling down Nelson's Column. Impervious to the rain, he walked along the glistening pavement. There was something cosy about the lights and the rain, a cosiness he couldn't reciprocate. The fear in him was cold yet calculated. He had made a treaty with it, and he would stick to it.

"Mr. John is here," said Micky, taking his overcoat off. "Where have you been?"

"I've been to the National Gallery."

"You should have gone to the flicks, then you wouldn't look so glum."

"Here you are," said John. "I've been waiting for you quite a while."

"You want whisky?" asked Miguelito.

"Not now, thank you. Miguelito, would you care to know the English countryside? Trees, hedgerows, green grass and all?"

"You are joking?" asked Miguelito, sitting down beside the electrically heated logs.

"And a real fire with hissing logs? No, I'm not joking."

"Where?" asked Miguelito.

John explained. From childhood onwards he had been friends with two sisters, both daughters of a long-dead Major-General. The mother had followed the Major-General ten years ago. The sisters, who were in their early thirties, lived on the Hampshire-Surrey border.

"The word border," said John the teacher, "should apply only to the frontier between Scotland and England or to a herbaceous one, but colloquially, my great pupil, you may use it when speaking of the strip of land that separates Hampshire from Surrey. Do you follow me?"

"No," said Miguelito.

"You will in time," said John.

The sisters had had a brother who was killed in the war. John had been at Winchester with the brother, which was one more reason why the sisters were fond of him. One of them, Angela, was a temporary civil servant in the Board of Trade; Jane, the other sister, bred French poodles. There was little money, but the sisters hung on to the Queen Anne house because, so believed John, they had nothing else to hang on to. They were unmarried, Jane was nice but Angela tricky. The poodles were sweet and barked at night less than you expected. They had never hit it off with Thelma. It was John's custom to stay one week-end a month with them, and he had telephoned Jane in the morning to say he was bringing a Spanish friend down with him for the week-end. Jane had no objection to it. Both sisters knew Spain, but, warned John, Miguelito shouldn't mention he was or had been a matador. They were the very embodiment of the society whose protection Miguelito sought in the British Isles. He was plain Mr. Miguel Pérez.

"I am glad to be Mr. Pérez," said Miguelito.

"And don't lose your heart at once to Angela," said John.

"I will not. If she is nice and wants to go to bed with me, I go and then laugh."

"I don't think she wants that. Both of them are virtuous as befits poor but honest ladies. Forget sex for the week-end. I hired a shabby car and now we're off. I hope it will be a change for you, Mr. Pérez. I will say you own a bodega. No, that's too alcoholic. I'll say you breed milch cows."

Miguelito nodded, Micky packed a bag, and the hired, shabby car joined the slow queue of cars struggling out of London.

"You will learn a lot this week-end," said John, watching a traffic light. "The country. You don't know what it means to us. Look at these mean houses, but those who dwell in these houses think of the hedgerows and of the monkey-puzzle tree. Every Britisher carries a monkey-puzzle tree in his heart." The traffic light changed. "The sisters have no monkey-puzzle tree. They belong to the impoverished ruling class who rather shun monkey-puzzle trees. Now we're in another traffic jam. Don't worry: there are plenty more to come. Miguelito, may I ask you a question?"

"Any question."

"Your English improves every minute. Tell me then

what role has Lolita in your life? I can't make it out."

"A man must have a woman," said Miguelito. "Perhaps not here but in Andalusia the sun is very hot. I like her body which is a very nice body. I can't say I like her mind because there is nothing there, but her body is often very sweet to me."

"Why don't you ask her over?"

"No, she is of my real life."

They were beginning to leave London behind, traffic was moving a trifle faster, then came to a jerky stop: a Labrador slowly trotted across the road.

"There is one thing I should like to see before I die," said John. "To see you fight."

"Never."

"I don't know. Micky said you were unhappy. I take little notice of it because for the Irish one is either blissfully happy or miserably unhappy. But I know your life is empty. If I could be as great in any domain as you are in yours I'd cling to it."

"I have no more greatness in me. Please, don't speak of the corrida."

You agonised Samson and you can't even pull it down, said John to himself, making a mental note of Samson for use in his next article. They drove in silence past identical houses, stopped to have a drink, and John advised Miguelito to have two or three drinks, for in the late Major-General's house it was unlikely they would have one.

"Why do you take me there?"

"I am fond of Jane and I should like her to see a good-looking man."

"No drinks, no sex, it will be rest," said Miguelito.

"A rest," said John, and they went back to the car.

"If this Ford hasn't seen better days then it ought to

be ditched," said John as the countryside began to prevail over the houses. "Trees and land," said John. "We are getting on. By the way the girls' name is Thorpe. The father was called Major-General Sir Lancelot Le Faure Thorpe, K.C.B., D.S.O., M.C."

"Why are you spelling?" asked Miguelito.

"Oh you are wonderful. Spelling? If the old fellow on the Day of Judgment isn't called by God with all his letters, then he just won't answer. Now, Miguelito, we are in the real country, approaching the border. It is a pity you can't see the conifers and the gorse. This is the most sinister part of England. Under the gorse lie murdered women who had previously been raped. Missing schoolboys and schoolgirls hanged themselves on the conifers, and the ponds round here are dragged daily by the police, and you may rest assured they find either chopped off thighs or old galoshes every time. Here we are. Alton is to the left. It was in Alton that my late mother whipped me for the last time."

The path, which Angela called a drive, came to a stop before the open gate, and the poodles in the kennels barked. Three poodles which roved freely were galumphing beside the car. On the doorstep of the ivy-ridden Queen Anne house stood an old man smoking a wet cigarette.

"Good evening, Scott," said John, getting out of the car.

"Good evening, Mr. John. Miss Jane is down at the kennels, Miss Angela has just got back from London. Have you the time?"

"A quarter to seven."

"That's nearly two hours overtime. I'll be off, Mr. John. Good night."

"England at work," said John to Miguelito, and took him into the house. "Angela," he shouted.

"Go into the drawing-room," shouted Angela in her studied low voice. "I'll be down in a jiffy."

They entered the drawing-room, which was like a china shop. There were Chelsea dogs on the chimney piece, Chelsea figures on the tables, a Queen Anne bookcase filled with Worcester plate, and in nooks and corners Spode had its say too. The late Major-General's medals were enshrined in glass; the late Lady Thorpe beamed in evening dress from a silver-framed photograph between two Chelsea dogs; the Wilton carpet was a little faded. A vast silver cup stood on an odious Dutch marquetry table.

"Bisley nineteen ten," said John, peering at the inscription. "Sorry, military point-to-point Darjeeling nineteen nine. Same thing. I am glad I brought you here. I bet the General missed Amritsar while he was on furlough."

Angela came in, wearing a black silk dress which swished too much. She was tall, her hair was black and her brown eyes were full of mistrust. One would have called her handsome at the first glance, but as her personality asserted itself one lost interest in her looks.

"Can your friend speak English?" she asked holding out her hand to Miguelito.

"Beautifully," said John.

"I am glad," she said. "I only speak English and a little Urdu. I don't think as a Spaniard you'd speak Urdu. After all you lost your colonies long before we did."

"I don't know what the Spanish colonies have to do with Urdu," said John.

"Do sit down, both of you," said Angela. "My sister, she my elder sister, she now soon coming, monsieur."

"From Urdu to pidgin English," said John. "Really, Angela, you are surpassing yourself."

Two chocolate-coloured poodles, both resembling Toussaint L'Ouverture, ambled in and sniffed Miguelito's shoes.

"Can we have a drink?" asked John.

"You know, John, that I don't approve of drinking, but Jane insisted on us getting a bottle of sherry. It's Spanish, for you, monsieur."

"Thank you very much," said Miguelito, wishing he had stayed in London and gone out with Micky and some Irish Kitty.

"You know, monsieur," said Angela, "we are here very insular, and you will have to forgive our very insular outlook and way of life, but that is how we are made. Here in this house where we used to have umpteen servants in the good old days my sister and I make do with one maid."

"Maid?" said John. "She hasn't got a maid, Miguelito. It's the old char Mrs. Wood who comes in to help when there are guests."

Angela gave him a furious look and John sniggered.

"Here you are at last," said Angela as Jane came in.

Curiously enough, the sisters resembled each other although Jane was fair with blue eyes and had a much sweeter nature. Both were tall, both had long legs and long straight noses, but once Jane began to smile and to talk, the resemblance vanished. She was an example of the spirit animating the body. Another broomstick, said Miguelito to himself, but nicer. Jane was wearing dark green tweeds and brogues, and four poodles came in her wake.

"How do you do?" she said to Miguelito. "I am so glad you could come." She had the gift of putting

warmth in anything she said. "Angela, has Señor Pérez
seen his room?"

"He hasn't," said John, "because Angela was trying to
make him feel as awkward as possible and . . ."

"I am afraid, monsieur," said Angela, "your friend
John hasn't much of a sense of humour."

"And no drink," said John, "but we've heard already
plenty about India."

"I'll get the sherry," said Jane, "and then perhaps,
señor, you'd like to see your room."

"Now, Miguelito," said John, "you must understand
that English country hospitality begins with showing you
the room, also by asking you whether you want to wash
your hands which means showing you where the loo is.
On the other hand, if you want to go to the loo you ask :
where can I powder my nose?"

"You are vulgar," said Angela but Jane laughed.

"In the morning your hostesses will ask you whether
you have slept well. Woe to you if you say you slept
badly. That would be shocking and very bad form."

"I wouldn't listen to his nonsense, monsieur," said
Angela showing a set of big teeth of which any camel
could have been proud.

"Angela," said Jane who had found the bottle of
sherry in a drawer of the bookcase, "why call our guest
monsieur when he is Spanish and you know how to say
señor as well as I?"

"For me all foreigners are French," said Angela, who
was beginning to hate Miguelito for his looks and
detachment.

"Actually Angela picked up more Spanish than I,"
said Jane, pouring out the sherry. "We spent two months
in Spain four years ago."

"A disastrous visit," said Angela. "Which part of Spain do you come from?"

"Lower Andalusia," said Miguelito.

"Then you know Seville?" asked Jane.

"Very well."

"I wonder," said Angela, "whether you know a horrible cousin of ours called Antonio Guada?"

"He is not horrible," said Miguelito, "he is my greatest and best friend. So you must be the cousins. He wanted to give me a letter for me to see you but then forgot. I am very glad to meet you but please he is not horrible."

"We don't hit it off," said Jane, "though I have a sneaking liking for him."

"I haven't," said Angela. "He is a traitor to his mother's country, and what does he do? Breeds bulls, bulls to be killed by those cowardly toreros. And how does he treat that poor wife of his, Maria? Like a servant. I think he is horrible."

Miguelito's right hand began to tremble. He knew the sign, and holding the right hand with the left which took on the trembling, he rose from his chair.

"You will excuse," he said, "but I will now go."

He rose, bowed, and while the three of them stared in astonishment at him, he went to the door, opened it, opened the front door, and with seven poodles around and behind him by now, he walked rapidly away on the muddy path known as the drive. His hands were still trembling.

"Señor," he heard behind him, "do stop por el amor de Dios."

Jane caught up with him, and as he stopped she put her hand on his shoulder: she was about two inches taller than he. The moon was playing hide-and-seek with the clouds; a cloud had caught her a short while ago but now she slipped away, lighting up the muddy path. Miguelito was moved by Jane's distressed eyes, which the moon had picked out.

"I am terribly sorry," she said, "but I beg you not to go. Angela didn't want to offend, she is just intolerant as all of us old maids are. The one thing I learned in Spanish when I stayed on Antonio's finca was por el amor de Dios. Please come back por el amor de Dios."

"I will for you," said Miguelito, moved, "but I cannot listen to words against my Antonio. He is more than a brother to me, and his mother she was my saint."

"She was our mother's sister," said Jane.

"Then I must go back to your house," said Miguelito, "because if you are the sobrina, I mean niece of Doña Mary then you are my good friend for life."

"Thank you," said Jane, "and we'll try to make you enjoy yourself this week-end." The moon was having a spell of glory with three clouds converging on her. "We needn't hurry back," said Jane, thinking how beautifully his face and hands were chiselled, and wanted to take his hand and bury it in hers. The moon lit up Miguelito's smile. "Let Angela stew in her own juice. She doesn't dislike you, she is simply furious because John rang me up and not her, so she didn't know till she got back that you were coming. Listen, let's walk to the village pub and have a drink. Come on."

They walked along the muddy path with the moon gone into hiding and the poodles behind them. Suddenly the poodles stopped, barked, then growling followed them.

"Por el amor de Dios," said Jane, "and the other I liked so much was que le pasa bien. You all say it with such sincerity. And adios, it's so sincere too."

"And the simple people—I come from the simple

7—SS

people—when they want to be not simple they say con
Dios if you say adios, and if you say con Dios they say
adios, because one must say something different."

"I think," said Jane, "we shall be friends."

What a pity, thought Miguelito, that she was so thin.
No behind, no belly, small bosom, in short nothing.

"Here we are," said Jane. "If we go into the saloon
bar we'll see the stockbrokers rustically playing shove-
halfpenny; if we go into the public bar we'll see
garage mechanics playing darts. We'll go into the public
bar."

In the public bar a game of darts was in progress, and
the players said good evening Miss Thorpe, and looked
with some curiosity at Miguelito. He asked Jane what
she wanted to drink.

"Cider," she said. "Standing beside you I feel shamefully tall."

"I shamefully small," he said, and she thought his
smile was enchanting.

"I want to explain to you our relationship with
Antonio," she said. "But do be patient and listen to me,
and try to understand our outlook which for better or
worse is different to yours and to Antonio's."

"But please nothing bad of Antonio."

"No, nothing bad. Let's sit down at that table."

They sat down at a table, that is sat on a wooden
bench side by side, and from time to time the buttocks
of the dart players almost touched them. Jane and
Angela had gone four years ago to Spain for a holiday,
and Antonio, since they were his cousins and he had
years before stayed with them, invited them to his finca.
The sisters went. Antonio was very drunk when he drove
them to the finca. That already upset Angela, which
Antonio couldn't help noticing, and he told them lewd

stories to shock her. It was never difficult to shock Angela.

"Relations were already strained when we reached his house," said Jane, "and then they became worse. Angela, like most women who can't find husbands, is a suffragette at heart, and saw straightaway in Maria the down-trodden woman, so she clung to her, was sweet to her, it was all the time Maria this and Maria that."

"I like Maria much," said Miguelito, "she is nice and good, but with the little I know now of your England I think you must understand that our women look at life differently from you. With a man in Andalusia are two lives : the house and the street; with women one life : the house."

"I know we missed a lot but there you are. We stayed a week, and Antonio did all he could to be unpleasant to Angela."

"Antonio is never unpleasant," said Miguelito. "He just pulls the leg."

"That's possible but Angela was downright unpleasant to him, and was in every sense Maria's clucking hen, spending her time telling Maria that no English woman would put up with Antonio who treated her just like a servant and so on. It wasn't a happy week, and I found it so depressing to see those poor bulls which would be murdered one day, and Antonio's friends came, and they talked and talked of bulls and bullfights. I was glad to go. Oh, I do hope you don't care for bullfights. Antonio wanted to take me to one but I refused."

"I don't like bullfights any more," said Miguelito.

"I am so glad," said Jane beaming at him. "I beg you not to bring up Antonio if Angela is about. To me you can say whatever you want."

"Antonio," said Miguelito, "is very good husband to

Maria. Her family was very glad when he married her. In Andalusia there are not many marriages of the heart. In marriage a man looks for mother for his children, and a woman for father of her children."

"How dull," said Jane. "Are you married?"

"No," said Miguelito and blushed a little, thinking of Thelma. It still rankled. "You are married?"

"No, I'm not, and probably never shall. I want too much from men and why should they want to give all that to me, a breeder of poodles with hardly a penny to my name?"

"You are very modest," said Miguelito politely.

"No," she said, "and now we'd better go back, and don't take any notice of what Angela says."

The clouds were quietly emptying their contents on the wintry fields and the muddy path. The poodles didn't think much of the rain, and owing to the rain neither Jane nor Miguelito spoke: they hurried towards the house. He was delightful, thought Jane, though she couldn't make him out. Not because he was a foreigner but because he possessed a form of serenity she couldn't probe; also there was something strangely dead about him, a lack of purpose, no desire to hold on. They had reached the gate when she said to him: "May I ask you what is your profession?"

"I have cows in Andalusia which give milk."

"They have nothing to do with bullfighting?"

"Oh no," said Miguelito.

"And why are you in England?"

"To know it a little."

"I wish I could know Spain a little. I know I missed an awful lot."

They found Angela standing before the fire in the

drawing-room. She gave Miguelito an artificial smile which implied she had forgiven and forgotten.

"I bet you've been to the pub," she said. "I for one have been to the kitchen. Mrs. Wood always loses her head when there are guests. I just managed to save the food, Jane."

"You are a heroine," said Jane. "I'm going to change now."

When they went to their bedrooms towards midnight John accompanied Miguelito to his room which sported china too, and on the walls were water-colours painted by the late Lady Thorpe. The room was bitterly cold. There was a knock on the door.

"I brought you a hot-water bottle," said Jane. She smiled at the two men. "You were bored," she said to Miguelito, "bored the whole evening. I could see that."

"No," said Miguelito, "but I don't understand what your sister she thinks."

"She doesn't think. I'll take you for a walk after breakfast in the morning. In the evening she'll go up to London, so tomorrow evening there will be only the three of us."

"Is she a virgin?" asked Miguelito when Jane left.

"I don't know but don't think so," said John. "Why do you ask that?"

"To learn English habits, John. I like her but she is too thin."

"She'd fill out for you," said John, and ripped a blanket off the bed. "Miguelito, I beg you, do me a *veronica* with this."

"No, never."

"Just once, I beg you. Please, please, please."

Miguelito made a deprecatory movement with his hand, then took the blanket. John watched him fold it, and when folded he held it against his body as he walked to the other end of the room. His gait had changed, he moved as John had seen him move in the bullring And Miguelito turned round, and as he was going to unfold the blanket which by now had become a cape he clearly saw a bull standing beside the bed. If he called the bull would come. He dropped the blanket.

"No," he said.

CHAPTER TEN

THEY WALKED in the cold wind across fields still wet from last night's rain. With him, thought Jane, she could walk till the end of the earth. She liked him for his smile and for the light touch of his presence. She had an instinctive dread of weight. He was light, perhaps almost too light, and she felt she should hold on to him so that the wind shouldn't blow him away. They reached a gate, she climbed over it, then Miguelito flung himself over it in less than a second.

"Good gracious," said Jane, "you can jump."

He wanted to say he'd had to jump the barrera often enough : he restrained himself just in time. "I like jumping," he said noncommittally.

"I've never seen anyone jump with such grace," she said. She must be careful : every minute she was liking him more, and he, plainly, was quite unimpressed by her. Jane wished she could look like those women with swinging hips she had seen in Seville and Jerez. Perhaps if she could swing her hips like them, and have as much flesh as they had, he would take notice of her. She gave him a sidelong glance : he was looking at rooks darkening the sky. They reached a high fence.

"We're not going through this fenced-in field," she said. "There's a bull in it."

"Bull?"

"A bull, a toro."

"I must see," said Miguelito and walking along the

fence they soon saw it, a roan dual-purpose Shorthorn bull, standing massively, its eyes turned in the direction of the two shapes on the other side of the fence. Then it started to graze.

"Elephant," said Miguelito. "For me he is no bull, too big, too much meat."

"Don't forget," said Jane, "we are the nation that built the Queen Mary. We like everything on a large scale. I must admit Antonio's bulls were finer in shape but this elephant, as you call it, at least won't be illtreated by a torero."

"By the butcher yes," said Miguelito. He threw his head back. "Eeeh, eee-eeh," he called.

"What's that?" Jane asked.

"I am speaking to him," said Miguelito. The bull continued to graze. "Eee-eh," called Miguelito, his head thrown back, his face lit up by the sun that beats down on the plaza de toros in Seville. "Eeeeeh."

The bull raised its head, and looked in the direction of the sound, then as he was going to return to his grazing Miguelito called again. Something, perhaps atavistic, stirred in the bull. Slowly he trotted to the fence where he stopped with his eyes glued to the two shapes on the other side.

"Ah-aaah-ah," called Miguelito. "So you have come, torito, you big ugly elephant." The light suddenly left his face. "We go, Miss Jane," and he strode away from the fence. Puzzled, Jane followed him. She'd had for a few seconds a glimpse of a Miguelito who was no relation of the man moving at her side.

"Does one call bulls in Spain like that?" she asked.

"Yes but different bulls."

"Fighting bulls, toros bravos?"

"I daresay," said Miguelito, who had become fond of the word.

"I suppose in your heart of hearts you Spaniards all love bullfights."

"I no," said Miguelito.

Rain, which had been waiting for an opportunity, now found it and poured down on them. It obliterated the clump of trees about fifty yards ahead of them. "Our beautiful English climate," exclaimed Jane. "Run, we must get under those trees."

She ran with two poodles barking in her wake, and as she ran she saw Miguelito running too but differently, with no effort, as though he were dancing. They reached the trees and they stopped under the little shelter the bare branches gave them.

"I am not afraid of rain," said Miguelito taking off his raincoat. "Your hair will be very wet, put it on your head." He lifted the coat.

"No, I don't need it," said Jane, but Miguelito put the raincoat over her head, arranging it carefully, taking her two hands, making them hold the coat over her head. So she stood with the raincoat canopying her wet hair, and he before her, but very near, his eyes on the raincoat. As his eyes left the coat, they met hers, and he knew he couldn't back out. He leaned forward with his hands hanging at his side, hers above her head with the raincoat and he kissed her. The violence of her response staggered him a bit.

"Kiss me again," she said. "Already last night I wanted you to kiss me."

He put his arms round her slim shoulders. It wasn't distasteful to touch those shoulders void of flesh. He didn't kiss her : he simply stood embracing her, and then it was her mouth that sought his. Her kiss frightened him; for no woman had kissed him like that before, and he felt as though she were taking advantage of him.

"You don't care for me a rap," said Jane, "but I care for you very much. I suppose every woman falls for you. Well, here you have one more. Don't look so shy."

"Perhaps we go now," he said.

"Already you want to run away? Give me one more kiss before we both get pneumonia."

The third kiss was more reassuring: it was a gentle, docile kiss and in gratitude Miguelito kissed her wet cheek and forehead.

"You are very nice," he said and meant it.

When they reached the house they found Angela in the drawing-room with the Sunday papers spread round her. She was sitting with angry eyes, a frown erasing the few looks she had.

"Here you are," she said. "Look, it's a quarter past twelve, and John is still snoring his head off. You know that Mrs. Wood is leaving at one, and of course she won't be able to make the room. As he is your great chum you'd better go and speak to him. Sit down, monsieur," she said ravishing a smile on Miguelito; for with sisterly instinct she had observed that Jane had taken to the Spaniard. She had noticed that Jane's lips were innocent of lipstick and was certain this had not been only the rain's doing.

"I'll get him down and then we'll go and have a drink, Miguel," said Jane, leaving the room.

"And how do you like our countryside?" asked Angela. "I love it."

"Very green," said Miguelito. "I like that. It has much peace. Can I please look at the newspaper?"

She handed him a bunch of them, her eyes in search of his; but he wasn't looking at her, only at the papers, and thus her dislike turned into hatred. She who hadn't the gift of love, loved to hate—which could fill her with rare passion, and give life a meaning. Sooner or later, she told herself happily, she would do him the dirty in some form or other, but like a patient lover she was willing to wait.

"Can you read English?" she asked.

"Yes, and I can look at English pictures too," smiled Miguelito.

Angela nodded: he was worthy of her hatred.

"You must get up," Jane was saying upstairs to John, "and I must talk to you."

"I don't really want to get up," said John. "I hate the country in winter." He shuddered. "I had a peep out when I got up an hour ago, and that sufficed."

"He likes it."

"Who?"

"Miguel. He says he likes it very much, he says it is very peaceful."

"I gather from your voice," said John sitting up, "that you've fallen for him. Beware, you have plenty of competitors."

"I am sure I have, John, but none of my competitors can ask as little as I. I am really hors concour. But tell me, who is he?"

"What do you mean, who is he? I told you he is Miguel Pérez, breeds milch cows and milks them, and has plenty of money."

"But there is more to him, I'm sure of that. We went for a walk, and in a paddock was a bull, and he called to the bull in a very queer voice, and his face was radiant as he called, and the bull came to him. The whole thing made a very curious impression on me. I suppose he knows bulls because he breeds cattle, but it was somehow different."

"A bull is sacred to a Spaniard, and that's all there is to it."

"I suppose so but I was glad to hear from him that he doesn't care for bullfights. I wouldn't care for a man who likes them. Anyway, he is too gentle to care for cruelty."

"Far too gentle," said John.

"Does he belong to a good Spanish family?"

"Well, he's a friend of your cousin," said John, who didn't want to tell her who Miguelito's parents were, as that would bring him too near to the truth. Besides, he was convinced that during their stay with Antonio the sisters must have heard the famous Miguelito mentioned. Enemies of the corrida, they probably paid no attention to it, but memory if tackled can dig up even forgotten nothings, so the less truth the better. He made a mental note to the effect that if Jane were to fall more for Miguelito than was good for him, he would tell her he was a matador which would end the matter abruptly.

"Does he like you?" John asked.

"I don't think so but as I've said I ask for nothing. The year I came out I had my first affair. Sheer curiosity, you know, but even then I knew at once I wasn't a man's woman, and Miguel, I'm sure, very much wants a man's woman. Now do get up or Angela will make life impossible for all of us."

Which she did till it was time for her to catch the train to London. She gave Miguelito her telephone number in Chelsea Cloisters and asked him to telephone her. Miguelito promised and resolved not to ring her. It rained into the night, and John sat reading and yawning while Jane chatted eagerly with Miguelito.

"And you are alone here all the week?" suddenly asked Miguelito.

"The whole week. Not really alone: I have the poodles."

"What do you do the whole time?"

"I read," she answered, flattered by his interest. "I am the typical indiscriminate woman reader. I read novels, I read biographies, I read books on history, travel books and then forget every one of them."

Now silence followed, with the rain's unobtrusive patter like a counterpoint, and the coal in the grate was soundlessly reaching its death by fire. Miguelito stood up.

"I like it, I like it very much. I could live like this, yes I could."

"Well I couldn't," said John, "and now I'm going to bed. Good night you two."

He read till one, when he discovered that he wasn't sleepy. He had heard them come up some time ago. He wondered whether Miguelito were asleep. He got out of bed, went along the passage and saw that Miguelito's door was ajar. The light was burning and the bed clearly showed that nobody had lain in it. As he stood staring at the bed he heard laughter, which had but one explanation, as it came from Jane's room at the end of the passage.

"Spain's gift to England's women," John said and went back to his room. At breakfast with scarce sunshine on the window panes he had to admit that the night had made Jane almost beautiful.

"Like a good boy," said John, "I've eaten my disgusting porridge. You, Miguelito, didn't have to eat it because as a foreigner you're not expected to—how lucky you are, and now we will have to be off." Jane's eyes clouded. "I'll bring him back some other time."

"Miguel," said Jane taking his small hand, "you really have nothing much to do in London. It means little to you whether you go up now or in the evening. Do stay the day if you can."

Miguelito was surprised and moved; for no woman had pleaded with him so passionately before, and he couldn't help thinking of Jane's cousins, Antonio's proud sisters, who would rather die than address a male like that.

"Thank you, I will stay," he said. "I do like it here." He took her hand and kissed it, and she leaned forward and kissed his forehead.

"I say," said John, and soon he drove off in the Ford.

He telephoned the flat in Jermyn Street in the evening, but Miguelito hadn't got back yet. Micky said if he had nothing better to do he should come round and meet two Irish girls. John didn't feel like romping with Irish girls, but telephoned next day again. Miguelito turned up only on Thursday evening.

"I like it," he said. "I like it very much. Peace, grass and trees, all green, and Jane so good and full of peace. John, I've known very little peace."

"Have you fallen in love and therefore am I going to lose you?"

"I am your friend for always. In love?" He shook his head. "I can't fall in love with a woman with a thin body, but I like her heart and soul very much."

CHAPTER ELEVEN

JOAQUIN'S FAVOURITE bar was in the Calle Tetuán in three existing children and with another ten or so to Seville. From his mean home, from his fat wife and come in time, he went to the bar, where he hung around till four in the afternoon when he would go back to his flat to eat. In winter he did little else than drink and play cards with his cronies. It was getting on for Christmas and the sun of Seville was in winter quarters. A pale grey sky laden with empty clouds seemed to sit on the top of the Giralda. Today Joaquin didn't feel like eating. He was full of wine.

"If I could speak to him," he said to two cronies, one a butcher, the other a carpenter who seldom worked, "I could persuade him to come back."

"How?" asked the butcher.

"You are a man of honesty and a man of heart," said the carpenter, "but frankly I don't think you have the gift of eloquent language. You weren't born to be a lawyer, take that from me."

"You mean I am dumb, eh? I can assure you if I want to talk I talk like a poet," said Joaquin, then drank wine. "Like two poets."

"Now then," said the butcher, winking at the carpenter, "what would you say to him if you saw him?"

"I," said Joaquin, pushing his chest out, "I would speak to him from my heart." The two men nodded solemnly though they were almost bursting with laughter.

"Matador, I would say, I am here, your Joaquin, your favourite picador."

"Excellent," said the butcher.

"Don't interrupt him," said the carpenter. "Something wonderful is coming, I've got my handkerchief ready."

"Matador," continued Joaquin in a pitiful voice, "you know you are of the lidia, because you are the great master of the lidia."

"Now that is really perfect," said the butcher. "Man, you express yourself better than the Quijote did."

"We miss you, matador, we miss you because we are your friends and we belong to you. Without you we are like orphans, you are our father and mother. Now what do you think of that? Isn't that good? Orphans, eh?"

"Joaquin," said the butcher, slapping his shoulder, "I was never so moved in my life before."

"And," said Joaquin, proud of himself, "I will remind him of the past. I will say: do you remember that bull in Bilbao?"

"What happened to that bull in Bilbao?" asked the carpenter.

"He unseated me, and then the horse fell on me, and the bull's horns got under the horse's armour, and he killed the horse on top of me. The dying horse was wriggling on top of me with the bull's horns tearing its innards out, and then there was complete silence, nothing moved any more, and I knew Miguelito had done the *quite*, and then they pulled the horse off me. I will remind him of that, and I will say I wasn't afraid, which isn't true, because I knew Miguelito would take the bull off."

"And you seriously think that would make him come back?" asked the butcher.

"Tengo siete iguales," shouted a blind lottery-ticket vendor, moving past their table.

"What he means," said the carpenter, "is to make Miguelito understand that if another horse climbs on him he would be squashed flat because Miguelito wouldn't get back in time from London."

"Mind you," said the butcher, "he could send him a telegram from under the horse."

"Just laugh," said Joaquin, "but if only I could see him . . ."

"Why don't you go to England? You have enough money."

"But I don't know where England is?"

"The trains do. I'd go if I were you. Joking apart I can assure you that with that eloquence of yours you could persuade him to do whatever you want."

"I only want him to come back, to serve him," said Joaquin.

"Then go," they said, and in the evening Joaquin waited on Antonio in the casino.

"What brings you here?" asked Antonio, and Joaquin explained why he came.

Antonio listened to the big, simple fellow and was deeply moved, understanding and appreciating the friendship and loyalty which prompted him.

"And you really want to go to London?" he asked. "It's far and for you it will be so strange, so different from anything you imagine."

"I don't want to see London, I want to see him."

"All right," said Antonio, making up his mind, "I'll give you his address, but swear on the Macarena you won't tell it to anybody, and if I were you I wouldn't tell even Manolo that you are going."

"I swear," said Joaquin, and Antonio gave him the

address, which Joaquin put into his wallet next to the photograph of his wife and children.

"Have you a passport?" asked Antonio.

"A what?"

"A passport, you need that to leave the country."

"What a pity London isn't in Spain," said Joaquin.

"Then Miguelito wouldn't be in London."

What with getting a passport and an exit permit Christmas appeared, which Joaquin was bound to spend with wife and children. Antonio had cautioned him to speak of his intended trip to nobody, and Joaquin, as happens with men whose brains move slowly if at all, was good at keeping his mouth shut. Only the butcher and the carpenter knew of the forthcoming expedition. Manolo didn't, nor did Bartolo the other picador, and it gave Joaquin infinite satisfaction to take a drink with either of them, he knowing and they not. After Christmas he went to a travel agency, accompanied by his two cronies. Alone he was afraid to face it. They explained he wanted to go to London, and the clerk suggested he should travel by air, but that was out of the question. Joaquin said he had been lifted into the air often enough for his liking, so a railway passage was booked, but then it transpired he would have to go by boat from Calais to Dover.

"Why?" he asked.

"England is an island," said the clerk, at which Joaquin was slightly perturbed.

The day came at length, in the first gusty week of January, for him to kiss his wife and children goodbye, telling them he was going to Bilbao. That bull, apparently, still preyed on his mind.

"Will you be away for long?" asked his wife.

"I don't think so, and you know I don't like to be

questioned. Anyhow, you have enough money to go twice a week to the cinema, and eat like horses."

"But you can't travel like that in the Taff," said the butcher on the morning of departure when Joaquin appeared in their bar with a small cardboard suitcase. He was wearing narrow grey Andalusian trousers, brown high-heeled boots, a grey Andalusian jacket, and a grey Andalusian hat with a black ribbon, also a short coat with a decrepit fur collar.

"I am going like this," he said, ordering drinks. "The English will know I'm not English because I don't speak their language, so let them know I am an Andaluz and proud of it too."

"Perhaps he is right to show himself in his true colours," said the butcher, and he and the carpenter shook with laughter.

"Besides," said Joaquin, "I'm not going to see the English, I am going to see Miguelito, and this suit will remind him too of his real country, of his real friends and of his true profession."

"You think of everything," said the butcher, and they bought him several bottles of sherry, and in the station buffet they drank till the silvery Taff with its Diesel engines and two coaches shook its way into Seville station. That was the moment for the butcher and the carpenter to become serious and to be moved by the imminent departure of the red-faced Argonaut. They clapped his shoulder, they embraced and said que te pase bien, and all three of them were deeply moved.

In the Taff Joaquin sat beside a gaunt American woman. He was already well filled with wine, pulled the cork out of one of the bottles, had a swig, then offered the bottle to the American woman, who gave him a frozen smile and a cold stare, so he shrugged his shoulders, offered the wine to other passengers, some of whom drank, while Joaquin beamed with the joy of the warmth of wine. When the steward asked him whether he wished to lunch he said he had fried fish in a paper bag and that would do for him. He ate the fish fried in rancid oil while the American woman toyed with chicken. When he had finished, and had spat the fish bones in a circle, he pushed the paper bag under the seat, by mistake touching the woman's ankles. She snorted and he beamed at her, then slept with his head nearly dropping into her lap. The passengers were mostly Andalusians, so they enjoyed the huge, red-faced man. He awoke in Cordova and said to the coach :

"I have been in the plaza de toros here more than a hundred times, if not two hundred, and not as a spectator either."

"I guessed at once you were a picador," said one of the passengers.

"I am Miguelito's picador," beamed Joaquin. "Have a drink, there's plenty more."

"I've read somewhere that Miguelito's gone on a long journey," said another passenger.

"He has," said Joaquin and laughed; for he remembered his meeting Lolita the evening before. They met accidentally in the street, and he, considering himself cunning and sly, asked her whether she had heard lately from Miguelito. Lolita said no, adding that it didn't worry her, so Joaquin shook hands with her, delighted with his unshared secret, and cantered off saying to himself if she only knew, if she only knew.

He was popular with the passengers and all his bottles were drunk by the time they reached Madrid, where he repaired immediately to the bar called Monteney in the

Gran Via, and after much finicky choosing with his eyes he picked up a fat woman because his ears heard her speak with an Andalusian accent. He spent the night with her.

He travelled third class to Irun on the next day, and was the life and soul of the compartment; at Irun station he ran into a friend from Seville, and after two drinks both decided to miss their respective trains, and caroused for two days, at the end of which the friend took a train to Madrid, Joaquin slept in Irun another night, and next morning a porter who'd had about fifty drinks off him put him into the Sud Express.

Soon Joaquin became subdued. The travellers spoke a language he couldn't grasp. It was probably English, and he sat in his corner seat staring at them moodily. They, after having smiled at his attire, took no further notice of him; and he arrived in Paris even more subdued, took a room in a hotel facing the station of Austerlitz, but cheered up when the porter told him he was Spanish, and from Jaen.

"That's Andalusia too," said Joaquin. "I am glad to meet you here in London."

"This is Paris," said the porter. "Now where do you want to go tonight?"

"I don't know this town."

"I'll get you a taxi and will tell him to take you to a Spanish restaurant on the other bank. There they will understand you."

They did. It was a small, rather scruffy place but the two waitresses were good to look at, and Joaquin chatted with them and tried to paw them. At the next table sat four bespectacled Catalans, serious and chatting in their own language in low tones. Joaquin was eating a *paella*.

"If you don't mind my saying so," said one of the

Catalans, "I think you'd be wise not to wear this fancy-dress here. The French will laugh at you."

"I am Spanish," said Joaquin, "and I will dress as they dress in my beautiful Andalusia. I am proud of being Spanish and Andaluz."

"That's nothing to be proud of these days," said another Catalan, taking off his spectacles as if to survey him better.

"I don't understand what you mean," said Joaquin.

They explained, and the table-to-table conversation ended with Joaquin calling the Catalans names. The proprietor, who was a Catalan too, told him to leave, but first made him pay for the rice.

"I am proud of being Spanish and you are all traitors," shouted Joaquin from the door.

"Get out or I'll call the police," said the proprietor, and in the street Joaquin still grunted indignantly. It was lucky for him that the porter of the hotel had given him a card on which the hotel's name and address were inscribed: he had forgotten its name. Back in the hotel he told the porter in no mean language what he thought of the restaurant.

"Take my advice," said the porter. "When outside Spain don't argue about Spain with other Spaniards."

"Argue? I don't argue: I just told those Catalans what I a Spaniard and an Andaluz thought of them."

"Precisely," said the porter.

In the morning an even more subdued and rather lost Joaquin entered the Continental Express, waiting resignedly for more trouble; which came in the customs' shed in Dover. The immigration officer could make no sense of the grey Andalusian suit. He hadn't seen one like that before, and found it highly suspicious. Moreover, the man didn't understand a word of English.

"What do you intend to do in England?" he asked. Joaquin stared at him, his face turning redder.

"Have you any money?"

Joaquin showed him Miguelito's address.

"I'll look at that later. Money?" and he showed him a ten shilling note. Joaquin understood and took out his travellers' cheques. There was, the immigration officer had to admit, nothing wrong with them. Eventually a Cuban volunteered as interpreter, and Joaquin was allowed to enter the country where his Miguelito was.

"And it is really true," said the Cuban in the train, "that Miguelito is in England and you're on your way to see him?"

"That's the only reason I am here. I don't like foreign parts. People don't seem to be gay, they have no alegria."

"With this rain what else can you expect?" said the Cuban. "And you just came to call on him?"

"I miss him very much," said Joaquin. "He really thinks of retiring."

"Now that's very interesting," said the Cuban, who was the Habana correspondent of a London evening paper and was on a short visit to England. "Very interesting," and he asked many questions, and slowly the picture he needed unfolded for his pen. He stood Joaquin two drinks, and drove him to Jermyn Street from Victoria Station.

"It's a big town, what?" asked the Cuban.

"Yes," said Joaquin, thinking he would soon be meeting his Miguelito.

He thanked the Cuban who wrote down the address, and when Joaquin, holding his suit-case, started for the first floor, the Cuban went to have a chat with the janitor, an obliging man well worth the outlay of half a crown.

Micky was sitting in the drawing-room listening to the wireless. With Miguelito's long absences in the country, life had become somewhat dull, so he answered the door bell at once on the principle that one never knew. He stared at the tall man in fancy dress.

"Well, I never," he said, "and who are you, if I may ask?"

"Miguelito," said Joaquin, adding, "Miguelito de Triana."

"You want to see the boss?" said Micky. "I'm beginning to understand Spanish, my friend. You come from Spain to see the boss. Got you right away but the boss isn't here. Come in, vamoos."

Joaquin followed him into the drawing-room, and he noticed neither the imitation Sheraton furniture nor the electric logs: he was looking for Miguelito. Micky took the cardboard case from Joaquin's big red hand, conspicuously red owing to the sleeves of coat and jacket being too short.

"Miguelito," said Micky, "he in country, not London, country. But I, savvy, now telephone. Look telephone." Joaquin moved to the telephone. "You sitty down, I get toll, savvy? Vamoos chair."

He pushed Joaquin into a chair, then dialled TOL, and while Micky stood with the receiver to his ear he surveyed Joaquin anew.

The man certainly looked quite out of the ordinary. Those boots, that hat in his lap, and those narrow trousers. The Spaniard, Micky had to admit, had made his evening.

"Trying to connect you," Toll said. Micky didn't bother to answer.

"It is you, Miss Thorpe?" asked Micky. Joaquin stood up and came to the telephone. "Please, get my

master to the phone. Somebody here wants to speak to
him urgently. Somebody from Spain." Micky could see
the urgency and excitement in Joaquin's usually empty
eyes. "Sir, a man in a very funny dress has arrived from
Spain to see you. He can't speak a word of English.
He's trying to push me away from the phone."

"From Spain?" asked Miguelito, his voice heavy with
foreboding.

"Here he is," said Micky. "I can't control him any
more." He handed the receiver to Joaquin.

"Miguelito," shouted Joaquin, and Micky jumped.

"Quien habla?" asked Miguelito.

"Me cago en diez," bellowed Joaquin, "it's me,
Joaquin, yes Joaquin, Joaquin your picador, your friend,
I am here in London in your house, come quickly, I
must see you, I've come a long way to see you."

"Joaquin," said Miguelito, "I can't believe it, man.
You in London?"

"In London to see you."

"Darling," whispered Jane who was standing beside
Miguelito. "What's happened? You've gone completely
white." That being as good an excuse as any she put her
arm round his neck. Instinctively Miguelito pushed her
arm away, then becoming conscious of what he did, he
patted the arm.

"He is from my farm," said Miguelito. "He says he
came to see me. I must go to London at once."

"I can't hear you, Miguelito," bellowed Joaquin.

"Go up in the morning," whispered Jane. "Please,
please."

"Yes," he said, "in the morning." He looked at the
china, the Wilton carpet, then at the logs and said to
himself it was all crashing round him, but he had been
childish to imagine he could cut himself off so easily.

"Speak, Miguelito," shouted Joaquin. "I can't hear a word."

"Send my servant to the telephone. He will put you up for the night, and I'll come and see you in the morning."

"Before I left," shouted Joaquin, "I ran into Lolita. She is well."

"I am glad to hear that. Joaquin, forgive me about tonight, but you'll have me tomorrow the whole day, friend."

He spoke to Micky who promised to look after and feed Joaquin, then he put down the receiver and stared at Jane, and then he asked for his London number. "I forgot to ask him something."

"Darling, you look so upset."

"Surprised. I thought he was in Andalusia, so you can understand my surprise."

"Please, darling, don't speak to me so aggressively and I wish I could help you, you look so worried."

This woman is far too good to me, thought Miguelito. Micky's voice came through the telephone. He told him to send Joaquin to the telephone. "Joaquin, does Lolita know where I am? I mean does she know my address?"

"She doesn't. Nobody knows, and nobody knows I'm here. They think I am in Bilbao."

"Who gave you my address?"

"Don Antonio but I had to swear on the Macarena to tell it to no one, and I told it to no one."

"Very good. Sleep well and I'll see you in the morning. But why have you come?"

"I am miserable without you and I wanted to see you."

"Dear, dear Joaquin," and Jane thought she had rarely seen his eyes so soft, so full of kindness.

"You look less worried," she said.

"It was a little shock," said Miguelito, and had the sudden desire to tell her the truth; but it was either too soon or too late; and if he told her the truth it would be asking for the end; if they parted he wouldn't suffer as she would, and certainly her goodness did not deserve this.

"If he is an old retainer of yours, why don't you bring him here tomorrow?" she asked.

"He has been my foreman for many years. Perhaps I will. We will see. Thank you."

Though Joaquin was drinking whisky in Jermyn Street, he was with Miguelito the entire evening, whereas Joaquin, having spoken to him, settled down to enjoy himself in the flat. Micky was doing him the honours.

"I must say you know how to drink," he said. "Just sit here and listen to the light programme, there are some good jokes coming, and I'll see if you have slippers. Those boots must be very uncomfortable." He was absent for a minute. "No, you have no slippers. You seem to have only these boots. I hope you won't sleep in them. What will you eat when you've had your belly-ful of whisky? I think I'll have a tot too. I'll cook you bacon and eggs. I bet you've never eaten them in sunny Spain, old man? But why do you wear that fancy-dress? Those trousers will burst if we don't look out. Take your boots off. They look too uncomfortable to me."

Joaquin sat grinning, his face purple, watching Micky, trusting him implicitly.

"I'll get you somebody who will talk to you in your lingo," said Micky and went to the telephone. Joaquin jumped up. "No, I'm not phoning Miguelito, so relax and sit down. Is that you, Mr. John? If you want to see a real Spanish he-man and have nothing better to do, come to the flat. . . . No, the master is down in Hants . . . since Monday . . . All right, I'll be expecting you." He put down the receiver. "Now, my friend, you'll be able to jabber in Spanish."

John arrived and after giving Joaquin one glance he asked : "Are you one of his picadors?"

"I am the first picador," said Joaquin. "I've just arrived from Seville."

"Why?" asked John in his slow Spanish.

"To see him. Are you, señor, a friend of his?" John nodded. "I came to speak to him, to tell him he must come back, he was born for the corrida so he must go back to it, he belongs to it."

"I see," said John and saw much else too.

"How long will you stay in England?" John asked later on.

"Till he comes back to Seville, but he will come soon."

"Do you think so? Tell me, was Miguelito ever badly gored?"

"Twice but not badly."

"Then why did he really quit?"

"It is like this, señor," said Joaquin, frowning in order to marshall his thoughts. "A torero retires because he has made enough money, a torero retires because he was badly gored and loses courage, a torero retires because he just loses courage, and his nerves go, or it is woman, or it is drink, but Miguelito's case is different. He ran away because he is afraid of himself and that's what Don Antonio says. He says Miguelito is so good, so great as a matador that he can't face himself in the ring any more. I am not an educated man but I understand what Don Antonio means."

"He says it's the bulls."

"The bulls are he. You've seen him fight? Have you ever seen anybody who dominates a bull like him?" John said no. "If he is afraid of himself then he is also afraid to dominate the bulls. I must speak to him to take his fear away."

"It will be interesting to see," said John, and they drank more whisky, and before turning in Joaquin sang an Andalusian song, which like most Andalusian songs, recorded calamities. The horse died, the donkey died, and the *novia*, the bride, went off with another man; then on top of it all the harvest was rotten.

CHAPTER TWELVE

"WE MUST get you another suit this very morning," said Miguelito as he and Joaquin embraced, pulled each other's ears, and then held each other at arms' length smiling with both of them near to tears. "Joaquin, Joaquin, to have come the whole way to see me."

"I had to," said Joaquin. "You must come back with me, and next season you will be fighting again."

"If you came for that, my friend, then you are wasting your time. I am finished with bulls."

"Matador, think of what it meant to you, to us who were your servants, your companions. Think of those days, say in Seville, when we drove to the plaza de toros, you sitting in the back of the big taxi, Luis beside you, the other two on the small seats, Paco beside the driver, and we two, your proud picadors, standing on the running boards, one each side."

"It's no good, Joaquin. I won't think of those days. Stay here as long as you want, I'll be very glad to have you; but when you go back you'll go alone."

"No, Miguelito, no," said Joaquin, wiping his eyes. He remembered the bull in Bilbao, and in a choking voice reminded Miguelito, who burst out laughing.

"What a donkey you are, Joaquin. I pulled the bull off by his tail."

"But you saved my life. Who will save my life from now on?"

"There are other toreros who know how to pull a bull's tail."

"Is this how you speak of our friendship, of the love we all have for you? You ought to see them. They miss you. When we are together we only speak of you, ask for your news. Miguelito, you must come back to us, back even to that awful Manolo."

"I will always be your friend but I won't go back to the bulls. And now I'll send Micky with you to buy you a suit like anybody else wears, and if you swear you will pretend to be the man I want you to be, namely the mayoral of my farm near Seville, then I will take you for two days to the house in the country of a lady whom I like very much. Needless to add, you will forget her when you go back to Seville. Now I will explain everything to you."

He was good at explaining and the simpleton that Joaquin was understood the situation in the end.

"But what will Lolita say?"

"If you don't tell her she won't know, and I know I can trust you. The lady is here, Lolita is there, and I don't want to think of the two at the same time. Besides, I like this lady in a very different way. Now off you go. Micky knows the sort of suit to get you, and you won't wear your hat while you are here."

"Miguelito, can't I sway you?"

"No, my Joaquin."

It was getting on for eleven, and soon John wandered in. They sat down, and talked of Joaquin's moving self-appointed mission, of Miguelito's categorical no, then the conversation drifted on to Jane, and from Jane to Angela.

"As I'm never there for the week-end I don't see her," said Miguelito.

"I wouldn't trust her," said John and the telephone bell rang. "That's for me, I bet. When I was in my bath this morning they rang up from an evening paper but my stupid landlady didn't know which. Now I'll find out. I hope it means an article." He sauntered to the telephone: since they needed him he needn't hurry. "Yes," he said, "it's Mr. John Thorpe speaking. Who? I'll wait. Hullo, Chris."

"John," said a nasal voice, "you're still the great bull-fighting expert, aren't you?"

"You flatter me."

"Now listen. Our Cuban correspondent is over here and he came in last night with a good story. A famous bullfighter is here in London because he has given up the fiesta brava—ha ha, I know a bit too, old boy—and is as it were in hiding from the bulls here in this country because here we have no fights. There's a story in that. Of course, we checked up on his story, telephoned our Madrid correspondent, and the man is really called Miguelito de Triana, and is one of the most famous bullfighters of our day. He lives in a flat in Jermyn Street, and I want you to go round and get an interview from him, and hurry because we want it for our late extra. There aren't many stories today. Photos we have, so I won't bother to send a photographer along. Get cracking."

"Yes," said John. "I'll ring you back."

Miguelito had gone from the room. John went and stood before the electric logs and tried to think, which was difficult, as he was no good in an emergency. When at last thoughts came they were focused on Jane, of whom he was truly fond; and she would in the long run be the one to be hurt. If Miguelito kept to his resolution, it mattered little whether the incognito was lifted.

But Jane, poor Jane—and Miguelito called from the bathroom, saying he was having a bath, for he had risen early and come into London to see Joaquin as soon as possible. John waited for fifteen minutes, then dialled the newspaper.

"Listen, Chris," he said, "the man's gone, left the flat, so I can do nothing about him."

"That's all right, old boy, forget it, though I should have liked to have a nice little bit from our bullfighting correspondent, meaning you. Bye-bye."

John felt clever, cunning, sighed with relief and poured himself a whisky and soda, for he knew he deserved it. When Miguelito appeared, he looked at him with steady, honest eyes. To please his friend, to prove his loyalty to Jane and to him, he had swept aside twenty-five guineas which he would very likely have got for the interview. Micky and Joaquin returned, and in a dark blue serge suit Joaquin looked like an outmoded giant.

"Hombre, hombre," said Miguelito, "you look elegant. I'll be proud to be seen with you."

"Let me be proud of you and come back," said Joaquin.

"If you start on that I'm not taking you to the country, and don't forget you've never seen a toro bravo in your life, but of milch cows plenty."

"I promised, so I won't forget," said Joaquin, thinking of his own eloquence praised by the butcher and the carpenter, and decided not to lose hope yet.

They travelled down by train, Joaquin taking little interest in the landscape : he had preferred the suburbs.

"Understand me," said Miguelito to him. "When I look at these green fields, at those grey yet curiously lilac clouds, then I know that here I can find a new life, a

life that will from now on suit me. Some, Joaquin, must
go on leading the same life, which after a time is bound
to become dull, but I in my new life, away from the
dust, sand and crowds you love—I feel as happy as a
child."

Joaquin grunted.

He bowed stiffly to Jane when they arrived at the
Queen Anne house, then took her hand in his huge
palm, squeezed it, and decided she was too thin and too
tall. Jane went out of the way to be pleasant to
Miguelito's foreman from the farm, which wasn't easy
as she had only learnt a few Spanish words from
Miguelito, but she gave him her warm smile, and after
a while Joaquin decided it didn't matter so much any
more that she was thin and tall. And Jane liked him for
the adoration in his eyes whenever he looked at
Miguelito. We both adore him, she thought, and probably John does too.

Miguelito took Joaquin for a long walk through the
fields, the gorse and past the ominous ponds. Joaquin
made no comments till he stopped abruptly and pointed
past the trees.

"A train," he said with satisfaction, "but what a small
engine. Is it because the English don't get enough help
from America?"

"I must say I did waste my walk on you," said
Miguelito, and arm in arm they walked back to the
house. Scott, the handyman, was on the doorstep. From
there without any effort he could survey the small
domain for which he worked as little as possible. He
handed Miguelito the afternoon paper, which it was his
habit to fetch from the station; this fitted well in with
his overtime.

"Here's the paper, darling," said Miguelito, giving it